W9-BDL-934

Fade Far Away

Avon Flare Books by
Francess Lantz

SOMEONE TO LOVE

FADE FAR AWAY

Francess Lantz

AN AVON FLARE BOOK

AVON BOOKS, INC.
1350 Avenue of the Americas
New York, New York 10019

Copyright © 1998 by Francess Lantz
Interior design by Kellan Peck
Visit our website at **http://www.AvonBooks.com**
ISBN: 0-380-97553-X

First Avon Flare Printing: August 1998

AVON FLARE TRADEMARK REG. U.S. PAT. OFF. AND IN OTHER COUNTRIES, MARCA REGIS-
TRADA, HECHO EN U.S.A.

Printed in the U.S.A.

FIRST EDITION

OPM   10   9   8   7   6   5   4   3   2   1

In memory of my father,
Frederick William Lantz
1908–1968

With many thanks to Elaine Spatz, Linda West, David Frecker M.D., Sally Owen, Mark Becker, Susan Jordan, Eric Tillinghast, John Landsberg, Gwen Montgomery, Renee Cho, and my wonderfully insightful and supportive writing group: Lou Lynda Richards, Mary Smith, Kim Gendreau, and Mary Hershey.

Prologue

Silence.

That's the first thing I notice when I walk into Hugh's studio. It's so unnaturally quiet.

The crack of my boot heels against the concrete floor sounds like a series of small explosions. I walk to the center of the room and sit cross-legged beside a neatly stacked pile of bronze ingots. The place smells of stale smoke and plaster dust. The big barn doors haven't been opened for days; the ceiling fans haven't been turned on.

Less than a month ago, this building was alive with sound and motion. Miles Davis blasting through the speakers as Hugh and his assistants, Eric and Mason, mixed plaster. The amazed gasps of the onlookers as Hugh lifted a crucible of molten bronze from the red-hot furnace. The grinding wail of the electric hammer as he broke open the investment mold, revealing the bronze sculpture within.

I had thought this studio was my father's version of paradise.

The place he felt most happy, most alive. How strange to find out it was really his prison.

I place my sketchbook on the floor in front of me. The cardboard cover is frayed and smudged. A few grains of sand are still lodged in the binding. "I've brought the island back with me," I whisper.

I've brought memories back, too.

I close my eyes and images assault me. Caleb's lobster boat bobbing on the gray-green sea, Hugh's face squinting into a Manhattan streetlight, hand-carved wooden flowers in the snow. My head feels light, my heart races.

I clench my fists and force my brain to go blank. It's easy to let the images overwhelm me, but I don't want to remember like that. That's why I'm here, alone, in Hugh's studio. That's why the sketchbook is lying at my feet. It will be my road map, leading me page by page, day by day, through the last two months. Forcing me to relive it all from start to finish, just the way it happened.

What the result of this exercise will be, I have no idea. I may never be able to make sense of everything that's happened, let alone accept it. Still, I know I have to try. I owe it to my father, to my mother. I owe it to me.

And so . . . I draw a deep breath and prepare myself. Sunlight streams through the skylights. The floor feels cold beneath my open palms. I reach for the sketchbook, open it, and begin.

PART I

The Farmhouse

Chapter 1

I'm in my room, trying to capture on paper the patches of sunshine and shadow that play tag across my legs. I put down my pencil and open the window, breathing in the warm, too-sweet smell of Indian summer. In a week or two the breezes will turn cold, and the handyman will come to put up the storm windows. But for now, I wear sleeveless tees to school and sweat my way through P.E., wondering if summer will ever end.

I finish my drawing and close the sketchbook. As usual, I feel a peculiar sense of relief. It's as if the things I see with my eyes somehow crawl inside me and start an itch I just have to scratch. Until I get them down on paper, I can't concentrate on anything else, can't distract myself, can't relax.

I stand up and walk downstairs, ghostlike, silent, hugging the sketchbook to my chest. Liesel, our housekeeper, is in the kitchen, making dinner. She's not from this family, not even from this country, but she seems to have a lot more purpose here than I do. She can make a soufflé, get micro-crystalline wax off blue jeans, and she knows how to brew that swampy herb tea Marianna swears gets rid of her indigestion. Marianna Scully is my mother. My father is Hugh Scully. I've never called them Mom and Dad, never even thought of it. I suppose it's because they never referred to themselves that way. I came fairly late into their lives—Hugh was forty-five, Marianna forty—and I don't think they ever viewed themselves as parents. They were too absorbed in the art world, and in each other.

I hear Marianna talking on the phone in her office. In December, the Los Angeles Museum of Contemporary Art is holding a retrospective of my father's work. As his business manager, it's her job to act as liaison between Hugh, his gallery in New York, and the museum.

"Did you speak to Kurt at the museum?" she says into the receiver. "Yes . . . yes . . . no, absolutely not. The pieces have to be freestanding. Look, have the inspector call me directly. Yes, as soon as possible."

I try to slink by unnoticed, but she's hanging up and sees me. "The city is trying to tell the museum they have to attach the pieces to the wall," she says. "Something about earthquake standards." She shakes her head as if stunned by their stupidity. "How was school?"

"Okay."

"I'm thinking of signing you up for art classes at Tyler."

"Marianna, no!"

"You're always scribbling in that sketchbook. You need to develop your talent, learn about color, design . . ."

"I haven't got any talent. I'm just screwing around."

"Well, it's about time you stopped screwing around and got passionate about something. What are you going to do after high school? Get married and become a soccer mom?"

"It's an option. Collecting coupons, getting my hair

done, maybe popping out a couple of kids . . . hey, I think I've found my calling."

The phone rings. Marianna shoots me a withering look and answers it. I take advantage of the distraction to head for the side door. I know she won't follow. She's much too busy.

I walk across the lawn to the high grass and into a stand of birch trees. Beethoven's Seventh Symphony is blasting out of Hugh's studio. I wonder what the original owners of this place would say if they could see it now. The farmhouse hasn't changed all that much, if you don't count the addition of electricity and indoor plumbing. But the barn—that's another story. It once housed animals and plows; now it's an art studio and bronze foundry. The place where Hugh Scully creates. The place where his heart lives.

I see cars in the driveway, so I know Hugh is holding an open studio. People wait months for the chance to watch him pour bronze. I'm lucky. I can watch him work any time I want, so long as I don't bother him or get in his way. So long as I remain invisible.

I open my sketchbook, study a slender, gray mushroom growing beside my foot, and think back to the first time I became aware that my father was famous. I was six years old, a precocious reader who viewed books as sacred treasures. I spent hours reading children's books, and hours more poring through the books in our house, searching for words I knew.

Then one day, in a fat, oversized book of pictures, I discovered my own name, Scully. I showed it to Marianna, who explained that what I was seeing was actually my father's name and that he was the creator of the sculpture pictured in the book. I was astonished, and so proud that my father had done something important enough to have his name in a book.

Now it's Hugh's talent that amazes me, not simply the fact that he's represented in books of twentieth-century art. But the feelings I had that day have never left me. I'm still astonished by him, and still proud.

7

The murmur of voices brings me back to the present, and I turn toward the barn. Hugh and his assistants have come outside, along with maybe twenty visitors. Hugh is pacing in front of the sand pit, shouting directions at Eric and Mason. I stand up and move closer, silently positioning myself behind a tree. Now I can see the wild glow in Hugh's eyes, the throbbing vein on his neck. His thick salt-and-pepper hair is mussed, his heavy leather jacket, apron, and boots do nothing to slow him down. As always when he's about to pour bronze, he can't stand still.

He motions the crowd back as Eric and Mason, wearing heat-resistant jackets and thick gloves, carry the heavy plaster investment molds out from the kiln. Using shovels, they pack the molds into the sand pit. Then Hugh walks to the melting furnace where the bronze ingots are heating. He waits while Eric and Mason don helmets with plastic masks that cover their faces.

Hugh slips on a pair of leather gloves, but his face is unprotected. He grabs the handle on the furnace lid and smiles in anticipation. The crowd can't take their eyes off him. Neither can I.

Hugh slides open the lid of the furnace, revealing the crucible of blazing yellow-orange bronze within. The crowd moves back, feeling the heat even from twenty feet away. They stare, open-mouthed, stunned by the color and consistency of the bronze, like Day-Glo liquid sunshine.

With Eric and Mason's help, Hugh uses tongs to lift up the two-hundred pound crucible of molten bronze. The crowd sucks in a collective breath as the men lug it to the sand pit. Slowly, carefully, Hugh pours the spitting yellow liquid into the first mold.

A moment later, the bronze rises in the vents and oozes to the surface of the mold. Hugh makes a fist and lets out a triumphant grunt. The crowd responds, exclaiming and applauding, but my father doesn't notice. He's moving on to the next mold, judging the heat of the bronze, deciding how long it will remain hot enough to pour.

Then suddenly, he grimaces and raises a hand to his head. No one notices except me. He takes a step, stumbles, and drops the handle that supports his side of the crucible. Eric and Mason stagger under the unexpected weight. The crucible falls into the sand pit, splattering molten bronze across the tops of the investment molds. At the same instant, Hugh collapses.

Someone must have dragged him away from the pit, but I don't remember anything except my heart throbbing, my breath coming in gasps as I run toward him. It isn't until I get there that I realize his body is stiff, his arms and legs are twitching uncontrollably. I fall to my knees, then hesitate. I never touch Hugh when he's awake and aware; how can I touch him now when he's so vulnerable, so not himself?

"Get Marianna!" I shout to Eric and Mason, surprised at the power of my voice. "Marianna!" I shriek, not waiting for their response. "Marianna!"

She appears a moment later, running out of the house with Liesel behind her. I back away as she kneels down beside him. She touches his shoulder and his body miraculously stops twitching, stops moving entirely. He's breathing deeply, eyes closed and mouth open, like a man in a deep sleep.

Marianna is scared, I can see it in her eyes. But as usual, she takes control. "Liesel, call an ambulance," she says. "Eric, please escort the people to their cars. Mason, clean up this mess."

She has forgotten about me, or so I think. Then she turns and says in a voice that's both reassuring and commanding, "Sienna, go inside now. Go on."

That's it. There's no job for me to do, no reason for me to be there. So I walk away. At the side door I turn back. From this angle, I can't see my father's face. There's only Marianna leaning over him, whispering intimate words in his ear.

Chapter 2

I'm sitting on a stool at the kitchen counter, drawing to keep from thinking. The distant whine of a siren grows louder as I sketch the tulips in the vase by the sink, capturing the shapes, adding the shadows. And then I hear the ambulance pull into the driveway. I'm scared to look, but I walk to the window. I don't know what I'm expecting—anything but what I see. Hugh is on his feet, talking to the paramedics. Marianna is at his side, looking up into his face, nodding, smiling.

The paramedics get back in the ambulance and drive away. Then Hugh and Marianna climb in the Range Rover and follow them down the driveway. A moment later, Liesel walks into the kitchen.

"What's happening?" I ask.

"Mr. Scully wouldn't get in the ambulance," she explains. "Mrs. Scully is driving him to the doctor."

"What's wrong with him?" I ask.

She frowns, considering. "It looked like some kind of seizure. Perhaps . . ." She shrugs, shakes her head. "The doctor will know."

I turn back to the window. Eric and Mason are reheating the bronze, preparing to pour it into the plaster molds that didn't get cast. It's a strange sight to see them working without my father. He's always nearby, giving orders, grabbing a shovel or a hacksaw and stepping in when he feels someone isn't doing things right.

"Come, Sienna," Liesel says, appearing at my shoulder. "I was about to make Mr. Scully an omelette. No need for it to go to waste."

I'm not hungry, but I let her lead me back to the stool. I want to be comforted, cared for, and right now this is the best I can hope for.

Hugh and Marianna come home late, after I'm already in bed. I hear them moving in the hallway and I sit up, straining to overhear some scrap of conversation. But they say nothing. Then I hear the door to their bedroom close and the house goes dark.

The next morning, it's as if nothing out of the ordinary ever occurred. Liesel is in the kitchen. "Would you like some pancakes?" she asks as I walk in.

I shrug, searching her face for clues, but she's as blank as a new sketchbook. If she knows anything, she isn't telling.

I walk down the hall to Marianna's office. She's sitting with her back to me, sipping coffee, and typing a letter on the word processor. I hesitate, wondering if I should speak. But I'm frightened of what I might find out. So I slip past the door and head outside.

The morning sun is golden; the grass is wet with dew. I walk over to the barn, then stop and listen. A Mozart string quartet is singing through the speakers so I know Hugh is inside. I lean my body against the barn door, letting the music wash over me and wishing I was listening to it at his side.

Long ago, I used to enter my father's studio as if it were my playhouse. That was when I was in preschool, eager and thoughtless and certain that the world revolved around me. Hugh was still painting sometimes back then, and I remember sitting on the floor beside him, scribbling with crayons while he worked. Even then my drawings were small and careful; even then Hugh didn't approve. He used to grab the crayon from my hand and tell me to loosen up, relax, think big and broad and bold. Then he'd fill the paper with color and line and hand it to me. "See?" he'd say. "That's how you do it. Now go on, Sienna. You try it."

So I'd start over, but the results never seemed to satisfy him. They were too timid, too monochromatic, too realistic. As his criticisms continued, my frustration grew, until finally I would throw the crayons aside, stamp my foot, and shout, "You're a bad bear! I don't like you!" Then Marianna would come and carry me, kicking and sobbing, out of the studio and back to the house.

After one too many tantrums, the barn was declared off-limits to me. I missed the smell of turpentine, the sun flooding through the skylights, the solid strength of my father standing beside me, doing important things with paint and clay and steel. But I didn't complain. In my four-year-old way, I understood I didn't belong there anymore. A test had been given me, and I had failed it.

Since that day, no one has ever told me to keep out of the studio. No one has had to. I watch from the doors, sometimes take Hugh a drink or a sandwich that Liesel has made for him, but I don't stay. I'm too old for crayons, and besides, my sketches are still small and careful. Only now Hugh doesn't disapprove. Now he doesn't notice.

Liesel's voice brings me back to the present. "Sienna, breakfast is ready."

I turn and head back across the grass. Marianna is waiting for me at the door. She meets my eye and my stomach tightens in anticipation of what she might tell me. But all she says is, "The bus will be here any minute."

"I know," I say. It's Friday, a school day. I walk toward the kitchen.

Then she says something else, speaking so softly I almost wonder if I've imagined it. "It's a brain tumor."

A sick, unsteady feeling floods through me. "What?"

I turn around to find her smiling. "It's not as bad as it sounds. We can lick this thing. Hugh's going to start radiation therapy right away."

"Radiation?" I repeat stupidly.

She nods. "To eradicate the tumor. Our goal is to get Hugh completely healthy in time for the opening of the L.A. retrospective."

She sounds so confident, so certain everything is under control that I don't think to question her, don't even bother to ask if the tumor is benign. It must be; the retrospective is only three months away and she said Hugh will be well by then, didn't she? Of course she did.

So I take all the questions, doubts, and fears that are spinning around inside me, force them into a little box, and close the lid. My brain is full of boxes, neatly stacked away so they won't cause anyone any trouble. One more won't matter.

I nod to show Marianna that I understand, that she doesn't have to worry about me, but she's already turned away and is walking back to her office. I wait until she steps inside and closes the door. Then I walk back outside, avoiding Liesel and the pancakes, and head down the driveway to wait for the bus.

Chapter 3

We're sitting on the rocks behind the library—Trey, Phillip, Carly, and me. The sun is shining, everyone is laughing. It's a day like any other—the same as last week, the same as last year, and not all that different from pre-school. When you go to private school, you have the same kids in your class year after year after year. You get to know them inside and out—or think you do.

No one really knows me.

"Miss Horkin looks even more repressed than last year," Carly remarks.

"If that's possible," Trey says.

"You think she's gay and doesn't know it?" Phillip wonders, biting the end off a stick of string cheese.

"I think *you* are," I say. "Look at the way you're fondling that cheese."

"Come out of the closet, man," Trey says. "We're with you one hundred percent."

Phillip picks up a pencil and flips it at Trey. Trey catches it midair and plunges it into his apple, then picks up the apple like an ear of corn and takes a bite. Funny, spontaneous, a little psycho. Just his style.

"What are you guys doing this weekend?" Carly asks.

"The band's playing at Lori's party tomorrow night," Phillip replies. "You gotta come."

"Can't," Trey says. "The play opens next week. I'll be rehearsing in Princeton all weekend."

"What about that soap?" Phillip asks. "You heard from them?"

"I got a call-back. It would just be a couple of lines, but hey, I'm not complaining."

Everybody around me is a creative powerhouse. They don't seem to notice that I have no discernible talent. Or maybe they just keep me around because I laugh at their jokes.

"Brush up on your method acting," I say. "Those soap operas are challenging stuff."

"Cruel vixen!" Trey growls, jumping up to take me in his arms. "Why do you taunt me when you know you adore me?"

Trey's yellow-green eyes are staring at me, but I look away. The truth is, he scares me. He's got some kind of flame burning inside him—I don't know if it's talent, charisma, or just raging ego, but I can't deal with it.

"Tell it to your fan club president," I say, hiding behind my I'm-so-bored face.

The bell rings and Trey releases me. We walk to our next class—Drama and Public Speaking. School only started a week ago and already I live in dread of that class. Why it's a requirement instead of an elective, I'll never know. Sometimes I wish I went to public school—someplace big and anonymous where no one would notice me.

"Let's talk homework," Mr. Firman announces first thing. "I want each of you to prepare a five-minute performance piece and present it in front of the class. It can be anything you want—a speech from a play or a screenplay, something you've written, a stand-up comedy routine, anything. Only two requirements. It's got to include words, and you've got to perform it live."

I can't do it, I tell myself. *I'll get up there and be unable to speak. Unable to breathe.*

I concentrate on the picture I'm sketching in my open notebook—the apple with the pencil through it. Images excite me, inspire me. I can make sense of them, organize them, duplicate them on paper. And when I'm finished, I can close the pages and stack them neatly on a shelf.

Words are harder, especially when they're spoken. They're like dangerous animals, unpredictable, powerful. The only things more revealing are bodies, faces. Especially faces. I never draw them, never look into them for more than a moment. They're weak fences that let the animals out, and let the world inside.

I think of Marianna, the calm way she told me about Hugh's tumor. The way she looked me in the eye. Words don't frighten her. Faces, either. I hear her voice inside my head. "Our goal is to get Hugh completely healthy in time for the opening of the L.A. retrospective."

She'll do it, too. I know she will. I only wish she'd let me help.

Chapter 4

Hugh and Marianna are in the office when I get home that afternoon. I hear their voices and start to turn away, but Marianna calls to me.

"How was school?" she asks when I appear at the door. The same question every day. The same answer, too.

"Okay."

I look at Hugh, half expecting to see a growth sprouting out of his skull, or bandages wrapped around his head, or *something*. But he looks normal, absolutely normal. Well, almost. He's holding a glass of mysterious green liquid in his hands.

"It's some kind of fruit and vegetable sludge Marianna has me drinking," he says, noticing my curious expression. "Delicious stuff. Here, you want it?"

"Stop that," Marianna scolds. "I've been on the phone all day, talking to doctors, dieticians, holistic healers, anyone who's involved in health care. The consensus is that natural, unprocessed foods can help the healing process."

"This stuff is giving me diarrhea," Hugh growls. "Is that part of the healing process?"

She laughs and their eyes meet. He smiles at her, takes a drink of the liquid. I feel their attention turning inward, away from me. That's my cue to leave. But today, something makes me stay. I want to be near them, to hear them speak and smile and react. To know that everything is normal, and Hugh is okay.

"We have to do a performance piece," I blurt out. "For Drama and Public Speaking. In front of the entire class."

"You don't mean a performance piece," Marianna says. "You mean a dramatic reading, don't you?"

"I don't know. That's what Mr. Firman called it. Either way, I can't do it."

"Of course you can," she says. "Ask Trey Cunningham to help you."

Marianna knows all about Trey's achievements. New Hope isn't that big, especially if you're a member of the artistic community.

I shake my head. "No, I couldn't do that."

The phone rings and Marianna answers it. "Yes," she says. "Uh-huh. Open studios are held the first and third Thursday of each month. We're usually booked two or three months in advance, so if you're interested, I'd suggest reserving a place now."

Pouring bronze requires energy, strength, timing. Pouring in front of an audience requires all that plus a sense of showmanship. It's not something a sick man could do, at least not competently. And what Hugh can't do well, he doesn't do.

I look over at him. His eyes are closed; the glass is empty. I let myself relax just a little.

That night, I'm lying in bed, listening to the wind fling the branches of the black walnut tree against the window.

I get up and look out. Everything is silver, glowing. The moon is full, but I can't see it from my side of the house.

I grab my sketchbook and walk downstairs. It's after midnight. The house is dark; no one is stirring. I walk outside and step barefoot onto the cool grass. The lights are on in Hugh's studio. Above the barn roof, the moon, surrounded by large, puffy clouds, gleams white. An owl screeches and takes off from a pine tree. I sit down on the cellar doors and begin to draw.

The whine of Hugh's electric hammer splits the silence. I pause, wondering what he's working on. Sixteen years ago, the year before I was born, Hugh did his first bronze pieces. He started small, creating delicate, highly polished abstract forms. Then he began casting bronze replicas of found objects—crumpled paper and aluminum foil, cans and bolts and string.

Soon after that, he created a life-sized bronze of a cluttered desk, complete with bronze pens and pencils, paper clips, checkbooks, and unpaid bills. The piece was a sensation. Critics loved the way Hugh had transformed ordinary objects into art, forcing the viewer to see them with a new eye. And they were blown away by the sheer amount of work that went into the piece, the hundreds of individual castings.

After that, Hugh's bronzes grew bigger and bigger. Soon he was creating installations—entire rooms filled with lifelike bronze objects. A bedroom with a double bed, rumpled sheets, a pillow thrown on the floor. A kitchen with a magnet-covered refrigerator, a sink full of dishes, a countertop with cut vegetables, glasses, an empty bottle of wine.

It's an amazing sight, walking into an installation like that. Suddenly, the things we look at every day, the things we take for granted, become unique and fascinating. It's a gift to be able to see the world anew, to discover pleasure in the mundane. Hugh has given that gift to people, and it's made him famous.

The hammer stops. I hear the sound of Hugh sand-blasting the plaster off the sculpture, then the squeal of an electric saw as he cuts off the gates—the framework of tubes that carry the liquid bronze into the mold. I get to my feet and move slowly toward the double barn doors. They're slightly ajar, as usual; even in the dead of winter Hugh likes the feel of fresh air.

I approach from the side, inching forward until I can peer through the opening. The bronze piece Hugh is working on is small, about the size of a basketball, but he's attacking it with the saw as if it were a ferocious beast. He cuts off a gate, kicks it aside, then cuts off another. Then all at once he lifts the saw in the air and slams it down on the bronze, sending the sculpture careening onto its side.

And now I see his face, half hidden behind a pair of eye protectors. He's tense, grimacing. He throws down the saw and flings the goggles off, then picks up the unfinished bronze and slams it down to the floor. It bounces off the concrete and rolls toward the burnout kiln. Hugh chases after it, then suddenly loses his balance and stumbles sideways. He rights himself, curses, and lunges for the bronze piece.

I gasp as I realize what's about to happen. Hugh lifts his arms over his head and hurls the sculpture straight at the barn doors. It hits with a thud, cracking the wood and sending the left door swinging open. I leap back into the darkness, but it's too late. He sees me and stares, his blue-gray eyes squinting into the night.

"What are you doing out there?" he demands, striding over to me.

"Nothing," I breathe, cowering against the edge of the door. "Drawing."

"You're always lurking in some corner, watching me. Why don't you and Marianna just leave me alone?"

The fact that he puts me in the same category with my mother confuses me. I don't know what to say.

"You know why that performance piece scares you?" he asks suddenly. "Because you're so damned uptight. I'll bet you've never been drunk, never gone skinny-dipping under a full moon, never filled a canvas with colors that take your breath away." He eyes me disdainfully. "You're probably still a virgin."

I stare at the gravel, my cheeks burning, too shaken to respond. I'm used to Hugh speaking his mind. He can be blunt, scathing even. But rarely does he express an opinion about anything concerning me. So why is he speaking now, and why must he be so completely, totally right? I don't know what it means to live life in bold strokes, to take risks. I'm not like him, and I never will be.

I want to escape, but he's watching me, waiting for something. A reply? Instead, I look over at the bronze piece lying on the floor. It looks like a rock, or maybe it's an abstract shape. And then it occurs to me that perhaps Hugh wasn't trying to harm or destroy the piece, but was purposely roughing up the texture, creating a specific look.

Hugh follows my gaze down to the bronze, then looks at me. For an instant, our eyes meet and what I see bewilders me. He looks troubled, uncertain. Maybe even scared. Then he frowns. "It's late, Sienna. Go to bed."

I stumble into the darkness, eager to escape his scorn, even more eager to avoid that unfamiliar uncertainty I saw on his face. Then I'm jogging across the grass, not looking back, snatching up my sketchbook as I hurry, breathless, into the farmhouse.

Chapter 5

When I wake up the next morning, the air is heavy and the sky is dark. I jump up, thinking I'm late for school, but then I realize it's Saturday and I have no place to go.

I stay in my room, fearful of meeting Hugh, until hunger drives me downstairs. The house is empty, silent, and a note on the kitchen counter tells me that Hugh and Marianna are in Philadelphia for a doctor's appointment. I think about the way Hugh stumbled last night when he was chasing after the sculpture. It was as if an invisible hand were shoving him to one side, forcing him to lose his balance. Was it just an accident, I wonder, or has the tumor affected his perception?

I walk outside, sketchbook under my arm. Black clouds are rolling across the sky. I glance toward the barn. The left side of the double doors—the one Hugh threw the bronze piece against—is open, and I wonder if I should shut it before the rain begins.

I take a few tentative steps, then hesitate. After my encounter with Hugh last night, the thought of going anywhere near his studio frightens me. I frown, remembering what he said to me.

You're always lurking in some corner, watching me.

He makes me sound like a ghost—a pathetic, needy ghost. Which is exactly how I feel.

You know why that performance piece scares you? Because you're so damned uptight.

It's true. I'm so closed, so timid that I can't even bring myself to draw with colored pencils. The burning intensity of reds and yellows, the icy chill of blues and greens—they intimidate me, overwhelm me. Black and white is all I can handle, all I can control.

I'm standing in the studio doorway now. The piece Hugh was working on last night is still lying on the floor. I stare, trying to make sense of it, until curiosity wins out over fear and I walk over and crouch beside it. Now I can see what it is—a bronze boulder, round and roughly textured, with delicate fern branches lying on it. And on one of the leaves, a small bronze spider.

I stare, fascinated. Hugh has never created a sculpture of a natural object before. All his installations duplicate man-made environments, interiors. I'm the one who sits out in rainstorms, wades through muddy creeks, lies with my nose in the grass, trying to sketch nature. I didn't think that kind of thing interested him.

I reach out and touch the bronze rock with its still-present gates and vents. I don't think Hugh was roughing it up. I think he was trying to destroy it, to smash it into a billion pieces. But why? If I could create an object like that, I'd never harm it. I'd cherish it.

I sit beside the bronze and open my sketchbook, overwhelmed with a desire to capture it on paper. To protect it, maybe. To save it.

I don't know how long I've been sitting there when the

sound of a car in the driveway makes me scramble to my feet. I know it must be Hugh and Marianna, and I know I can't let them find me here. I hurry to the doors, then freeze when I hear their voices.

"Show me what you were working on last night."

"It's not polished yet."

"Polish it now."

"I feel exhausted. How am I going to make it through two months of these damned radiation treatments?"

"The time will pass quickly, you'll see."

"You're going to have to cancel the open studios," he says. "People aren't paying to watch me puke."

Marianna laughs softly. "You'll be all right. You've got to stay focused, keep working. You're going to get better. I know it."

"*How* do you know?"

"Because you *have* to get better. You've got so many things still to do, so much to create. This new installation is going to take you to a whole new level."

"Maybe."

"It is. Look, go lie down. I'll wake you in an hour. Then you can take your vitamins and get back to work."

A pause, then a sigh. "You're right. You're always right."

I hear their footsteps on the gravel growing softer as they head toward the house, and I edge up to the barn doors to watch. She's got her arm around his waist, her hip against his. His legs seem a bit unsteady but he's standing tall, head held high.

I wonder how Marianna would react if she knew what had happened last night, if she knew he'd slammed the bronze rock against the floor, hurled it at the door. Would she be shocked? Appalled? Frightened?

No. She would understand immediately, would know what he was feeling, what he was needing. She'd hold him, soothe him, then tease and scold him—whatever it took to diffuse his anger. To get him back to work. And he would respond—not with fury, but with gratitude. Because he needs her. Because he loves her.

What I wouldn't give to be able to do that for someone. To be listened to like that, to be needed. What I wouldn't give to be loved.

Chapter 6

The rain comes hard and long, flooding the basement and splashing through the screens to drench the windows. When it ends, the temperature drops, turning the leaves red and yellow around the edges. Canada geese fly in formation over the Delaware, and suddenly the farmstands are overflowing with pumpkins and Indian corn.

I spend the next three weeks laying low, trying not to get in Hugh's way. School takes up the days, and I spend the evenings in my room, laboring over my homework, checking and doublechecking my answers. On weekends, I head for the damp cornfields behind our house, and beyond that, the woods. I hike, sketch, and try not to think about Hugh's thinning face, his dark moods, or the way he walked into the edge of the barn door during the last open studio.

Finally, the day comes for me to do my performance piece. I've avoided thinking about it for weeks; I'm completely unprepared. The night before, I select a story by Dorothy Parker called "The Waltz"—the secret, unspoken thoughts of a woman who is asked to dance by an unwanted suitor.

But of course I don't do it justice. My mouth is dry and my palms are damp. I mumble, trip over words, and Mr. Firman asks me to speak up again and again. Inside, I'm the protagonist of the story. All sorts of cutting remarks come to me—about Mr. Firman, who confuses making eye contact with making art, about the students, about me. But on the outside, I'm red-faced, apologetic. When it's all over, Mr. Firman takes pity on me and gives me a C.

It's the beginning of October, a golden autumn morning. I walk down the hallway to the bathroom and see Marianna in her bedroom, packing her bags. It's not unusual for Hugh and Marianna to go out of town for an opening, leaving me with Liesel for two or three days. But no one has said anything to me about a trip happening now, today.

Marianna stops, feeling my eyes on her, and turns around. "I'm going to L.A. to supervise the setup of the installations," she explains. "I'll be back in less than a week."

Now I'm really confused. How can she go without Hugh? "You're going alone?" I ask.

"Hugh will go out later. Maybe next month."

There's so much I want to ask, but I don't know where to start, don't know if my questions will be welcome. Finally, all I manage to say is "How is he?"

"He's working, that's the important thing. He's staying on track."

She goes back to packing, and I know she doesn't want to talk about it any more. But I can't leave.

"He's losing weight," I say at last.

"He'll gain it back. We've stopped the radiation. It causes more problems than it solves."

"But what—?" My voice trails off. I don't know what I want to ask.

"I'm studying alternative therapies," she says. "The body can cure itself if conditions are right."

She looks at me defiantly, as if daring me to disagree. But all I feel is relief. My mother is a woman who makes things happen. She's guided Hugh's career from the beginning, inspired and encouraged him to grow as an artist, as a man. Now she's guiding him on another journey, from sickness back to health.

It's Monday evening. Marianna has been gone since early this morning. I'm in my room, cleaning out my desk drawers to avoid doing my geometry homework. Carly calls and we talk about a piece she's writing for the underground paper she edits, whether she should henna her hair, the relative merits of Johnny Depp versus Brad Pitt.

When she hangs up, I go downstairs for a soda. I walk through the living room and stop, startled to find Hugh at the dining room table. I suppose I shouldn't be—it's seven o'clock, Hugh and Marianna's usual dinnertime—but I'd assumed since she wasn't here, he'd be in the studio working.

"I'm sorry," I say, edging sideways toward the kitchen.

"Why?"

"I don't want to bother you. I'm just getting a drink."

"You ate already?"

I nod. Liesel always fixes me something in the kitchen around six o'clock. Hugh and Marianna like to eat together, a relaxed meal with candlelight, wine, conversation. Sometimes friends stop by for espresso and chocolates.

"You want a glass of wine?" he asks.

"No. Thanks. I've got homework."

I hurry into the kitchen and take a soda from the refrigerator. Liesel is cleaning up. "I made a linzer torte. Do you want a piece?"

What I want is to get back to my room, my safe little world. I shake my head and shuffle back through the dining room, but I can't help glancing at Hugh. His shoulders are hunched, the left side a bit lower than the right. He looks small and alone at the end of the long oak table.

"Sienna," he says softly.

I pause.

"That night outside the studio. I'm sorry about what I said. That was uncalled for."

I turn, shrug. "But true."

"Really?" He looks surprised, a little amused. "Then get out there and start living. What are you afraid of?"

"Nothing. Everything." Another shrug. "You wouldn't understand."

He takes a sip of wine, looks into the glass. "I understand fear," he says, so softly I'm not sure I heard him correctly. I wait for him to say more, but he finishes off his wine and pushes back his chair. "I'll be in the studio if you need me."

"Okay. Sure."

He stands up, walks to the kitchen door and glances back at me. We gaze at each other, awkwardly, like strangers. Part of me longs to say something, any foolish thing that will make him stay a moment longer. Another part of me wants to run. But before I can do anything, he turns and strides through the door—purposeful, intent—and I know he's no longer thinking about me.

Chapter 7

The next afternoon, the bus lets me off at the end of the driveway and I walk toward the house, pausing to sketch the neighbor's cat, Samantha, stretched out across the gravel in a patch of sunlight. Eric is at the top of the drive, getting into his purple Gremlin. Behind him, the studio doors are wide open. I wave to him and walk across the gravel to the house.

"Sienna?"

I turn to see Hugh, a welding helmet pushed up on his forehead, motioning to me from inside the studio. I walk through the double doors and join him at the welding table. On it are two three-foot-tall sections of bronze tree trunk, one resting on top of the other.

"Eric had to leave," he says. "Hold this piece steady while I weld it, will you?"

I put my books on the floor and watch while he lines up the sections so the edges are flush. "Here, put these on." He hands me a pair of leather gloves and a helmet. I do as I'm told, feeling foolish but excited. Hugh has never asked me to help him before, never involved me in his work.

He shows me where to hold the sections, then lowers his helmet. He picks up the welding gun and pulls the trigger, igniting a spark. I look away, startled by the intense blue-green flame. There's a sound like bacon frying, then, after about a minute, silence.

"You can let go now."

I step back, raise my helmet and look at the sections, now welded together into one piece of trunk. The bark is intricate, so real, but metallic, gleaming. "It's beautiful," I tell him.

He puts down the welding torch. "I must have been crazy to promise a new installation for the retrospective. It's too big, too involved. I don't know what I'm doing."

"It's not an interior."

"No, I couldn't do another room. This is something new. A forest."

"Wow," I breathe, and immediately feel like an idiot. I sound like a five-year-old.

I glance anxiously at Hugh, expecting him to cut me down with a word, a look. But his eyes are closed tight, his forehead is furrowed, his teeth clenched. I turn away, not wanting to see him looking weak, in pain; not knowing what to say or do.

He lets out a long breath. "My head is throbbing. Can you get me some aspirin and a cup of coffee?"

I nod, feeling better now that I have something to do. I run into the house, get aspirin from the downstairs bathroom, then go into the kitchen. It's Liesel's afternoon off but there's half a pot of coffee in the coffeemaker. I pour a cup, then have an idea. I put ice water in a pot and grab some hand towels. I put everything on a cutting board and carry it back to the studio.

"I thought cold compresses might help," I say by way of explanation.

He raises his eyebrows, then smiles. "Thanks." He puts the aspirin in his mouth and throws back his head, washing them down with coffee. "I'm going to lie down just for a minute," he says, as if he's expecting an argument. "Then I'll get back to work."

There's a cot set up near the sink. I never noticed it before; maybe it's new. I watch him walk toward it. With each step, his left foot drags ever so slightly on the concrete.

I set the cutting board on the floor beside the cot. "I'll be in the house if you need me," I say, then pause. I wish I could stay, but there's no reason.

He nods, waiting for me to leave. So I go, feeling lightheaded and inexplicably happy.

I don't see Hugh again until the next evening. I'm eating dinner at the kitchen counter when he walks in.

"What's that?" he asks, squinting at my plate.

"Pasta Primavera," Liesel answers. "Would you like some, Mr. Scully?"

"Why not?" He looks at me. "Let's eat in the studio. I've got work to do." He turns and walks out of the room.

"Go on," Liesel says. "I'll bring his dinner."

I grab my plate and my soda and hurry out to the studio. Hugh is already there, using a wire brush to remove plaster investment from a section of bronze tree trunk. On the floor are branches and leaves from real trees, along with blocks of plastic-wrapped modeling clay.

"How's your head?" I ask, sitting on a stool to watch him work.

"Lousy. How's yours?"

He's silenced me, as I guess he knew he would. We don't say anything until Liesel appears with a plate of pasta, a salad, and a glass of wine. She puts them on the welding table and leaves.

Hugh takes a bite. "Too healthy," he says. "You know what I'd really like? Macaroni and cheese. The kind my mother used to make, with breadcrumbs and lots of butter."

I wonder what it's like to have a mother who cooks for you. One who vacuums and does laundry and changes sheets. It wouldn't be so tough to emulate a mother like that, to feel that someday I could be just as clever, just as capable.

"I guess that wouldn't fit into your new diet," I say.

He nods. "I suppose it's helping me. I don't know. Marianna seems to think so." He takes a long sip of wine, then another. "Come here, Sienna. I want to show you something."

He leads me to a corner of the studio, where huge sheets of off-white canvas have been hung from the ceiling, creating a giant curtain. He pulls the corner of the canvas aside, revealing the trunk of a life-sized bronze tree. Slowly, I look up. There must be ten or twelve of them—twenty-foot-high bronze trees, complete with slender branches and hundreds of delicate leaves.

"So tell me—what would you think if I used these trees and then filled out the rest of the installation with bushes and saplings?"

I hesitate, unable to believe he's asking me to comment on his work. "I . . . I don't know," I stammer. "What are you trying to create?"

"Originally, I envisioned something huge—a bronze forest big enough to get lost in." He throws his arms out wide and I picture it along with him—a pristine metallic forest, familiar yet weirdly alien. The thought takes my breath away.

"It was an interesting idea," he says, "but I can't finish in time for the retrospective unless I scale down my vision." He frowns, gazes into the middle distance. "Okay, here's another idea—make the whole thing three-quarter size. Would that lessen the impact?"

Yes, I think, then immediately push the thought aside. Who am I to criticize Hugh's work? "Whatever you decide will be the right choice," I say, and I mean it. "You know the effect you're going for."

"What a load of crap," he growls. "You don't have to humor me because I've got a lump growing inside my head. Just speak your mind."

What does he want me to say? Does he hate the idea of scaling down the installation? Is he hoping I'll tell him he's making a mistake? That's what Marianna would say—at least I imagine it is.

"Your installations have always been life-sized and detailed," I say at last. "If you make this one anything less, it will seem like a cop-out."

He stares at me, his eyes hard. "I don't think you understand what I'm trying to do," he says coolly. "This isn't about impressing people with my ability to create perfect replicas of real life. If I wanted that, I'd do celebrity portraits."

He turns away, grabs the wire brush and goes back to work. It feels like he's scraping me clean, exposing all my stupidity and inadequacy. I wolf down my pasta with my stomach churning, then grab my plate and move toward the door, desperate to escape.

"Sienna."

I stop short. "Yes?"

"You're right. If I do this thing half-assed, everyone will know it. *I'll* know it."

My heart soars. "Are you sure? I don't really know what I'm talking about."

"I think you do. A three-quarter scale forest would be a disaster. This isn't a model railroad I'm building."

"I keep thinking trolls."

"What?"

"If you build it small, it will look like a fantasy forest, like with trolls or leprechauns or something."

He stares at me, then bursts out laughing, a deep, rich laugh that fills the studio. "God, you nailed it, Sienna. Maybe I could add a few lawn jockeys, too."

I giggle, and then we're both laughing. It's something I haven't done with him very often. It feels good.

When the laughter ends, the silence returns. He goes back to work, ignoring me again, but I don't care. I feel excited, giddy. I leave the studio and grin up at the setting sun, the pale moon, the lovely orange sky.

Chapter 8

When I get home from school the next afternoon I go immediately to the studio, hoping to find Hugh there. What I find is Hugh and Marianna standing on opposite sides of the welding table, talking quietly.

Hugh looks up; Marianna notices and turns around. She walks over and kisses my cheek. "Hello, Sienna."

"When did you get back?" I ask, trying not to show my disappointment. Trying not to feel it.

"Just an hour ago. Everything went well. The installations look fabulous. I even got things straightened out with the earthquake standards people."

"Good." I glance at Hugh. He's leaning over, palms flat against the table, eyes closed. I wonder if his head hurts, but I don't ask. Marianna will take care of him.

She smiles at me again but says nothing. She's waiting for me to leave, I know. So I do, clutching my books to my chest as I turn away.

I'm flat on my stomach on a blanket of brilliant red and yellow leaves, sketching a wren hopping among the chrysanthemums, when I hear Marianna's voice.

"Sienna, what are you doing?"

I jump to my knees, spin around. "Nothing."

She looks over my shoulder at the sketchbook, still lying open in the grass. "You'll make a good illustrator someday."

I close the sketchbook. I know what she thinks of illustrators. They aren't artists. "What do you want?"

"We need to talk."

I reach for my sketchbook, stand up, wait. Did Hugh tell her I was in his studio while she was gone? Is she going to reprimand me for disturbing him, for keeping him from his work?

"Hugh's starting a new diet," she says. "It's going to be very demanding—twelve glasses of raw pressed fruit and vegetable juices daily, no meat, salt, sugar. No bottled, frozen, or preserved foods. Enemas every four hours to cleanse the system. I did some research while I was in California and I'm very optimistic."

"He's having headaches."

She nods. "It's fluid buildup from the tumor. The doctor wants to give him drugs, but I don't know. We have to make a choice. If we let them put chemicals into his body, it will negate the potential benefits of the diet."

I know the "we" Marianna is referring to doesn't include me, so I don't say anything. In any case, what *could* I say? I have no idea what's best for Hugh, not a clue what he needs.

"I'd like to ask you a favor, Sienna. Don't eat where Hugh can see you. It's going to be hard enough for him to stick to the diet. I don't want him to be tempted by forbidden foods."

"Maybe I should go on the diet, too," I suggest.

She smiles. "Thank you. That's very thoughtful, but I don't want to put you through it. It's not the sort of diet a teenager—or anyone, really—would choose to follow. But if it gets results . . ."

"I just want to help."

"You *are* helping. I'll ask Liesel to bring your meals up to your room—just for a while, until we see how your father responds to the diet."

I nod. "All right."

She reaches out, gently squeezes my shoulder, then turns and walks away.

Eating in my room turns out to be easier than I'd imagined. I spend hours listening to music with my headphones on, sketching, doing homework, reading. The days pass by. It's not so bad.

But sometimes I think about what happened while Marianna was in L.A. I see myself in the studio, standing side-by-side with my father, gazing up at the huge sculpted trees. I remember the way he listened to me, resisted, then thought it over. I hear him laughing, telling me, "You really nailed it, Sienna." Like what I thought mattered. Like he really cared about my opinion.

And then I tell myself that those few days were a fluke, an anomaly. Without Marianna to encourage and guide him, with his headaches raging, Hugh needed someone to talk to, someone to comfort him, to reassure him that his work was meaningful and valid. That someone just happened to be me. For all I know, he may have discussed his latest installation with Eric, with Mason, with any number of fellow artists and friends. He probably phoned Marianna in L.A. as well. I shouldn't think I'm so special.

Still, when I pass the barn one brisk, overcast Saturday afternoon and hear the white noise of a fan punctuated by the hissing of a welding torch, I find myself slowing down, stopping, inching toward the half-opened door. Hugh is standing at the table, attaching delicate bronze leaves to a bronze tree branch. No one is helping him, no one is holding the pieces. I feel my heart leap into my throat as I think, *He didn't need my help. He wanted it. He chose to have me with him.*

Would he feel the same way now? I wonder. My chest feels tight, my stomach is fluttering. I hesitate, my fingers on the door. At that moment, his left hand—the one holding the leaves in place—goes limp and drops into the path of the flame. He gasps with pain, drops the welding torch, and staggers backward, using his good hand to fling off his goggles.

In an instant, I'm throwing open the barn door and running toward him. But before his goggles hit the floor, Marianna appears from behind the burnout oven and grabs him, helps him regain his balance, then takes his hand and studies the injury. As for me, I'm standing motionless somewhere between the door and the welding table, wondering what Marianna is doing in the studio while Hugh is working, wondering what makes me think I have the right to question her presence, now or ever.

Hugh's wound must be slight because Marianna hugs him, then reaches up to slip her arm around his waist and lead him toward the cot. I watch, holding my breath, then slip silently through the doors and out into the afternoon grayness. I don't know if they've seen me, heard me—if they even knew I was there at all. All I know is I'm alone, and so lonely.

Chapter 9

"What's your pleasure, Trey?" Lori asks. "Beer or weed?"

"I've got two hands. Why choose?"

In the corner, Phillip's band, Radiator, is tuning up. It's Saturday night, just hours after I ran out of Hugh's studio unnoticed, and I'm peering across Lori's dim basement, watching a couple dozen kids laughing and talking and getting high. Lori is famous for her parties, always held when her parents are out of town. Carly's been telling me about them for months, but I've never gone. Never wanted to. So why am I here tonight?

Maybe because I won't let myself spend another evening crouching in the shadows at the top of the stairs, trying to catch a bit of Hugh and Marianna's dinner conversation. Because I can't take another night lying awake in bed, wondering why my father looks thinner than he did a month ago, why he walks into walls and burns himself welding, why, despite Marianna's insistence to the contrary, he doesn't seem to be getting better.

The squeal of feedback. The click of drumstick against drumstick. Then Radiator begins to play. It's an angry song, with grinding guitars, a pounding rhythm, and Phillip's voice growling through the sound system. It feels right, so right, and I close my eyes and let the music pour into me and fill me up.

When it ends, Trey is standing next to me, holding out a bottle of beer. I don't let myself think; I just take it and drink. He grins, then grabs my hand and pulls me into the center of the room. The music starts again and we're dancing—or actually *he's* dancing, I'm just swaying a little, trying not to look as horribly self-conscious as I feel.

He watches me, laughs, then leans over to whisper in my ear. "You're a mystery, Sienna. Are you totally uncool, or way too cool to bother?"

"Too cool to bother with the likes of you," I shout over the music.

A tall guy I've never seen before hands Trey a joint. He takes a hit and offers it to me. I shake my head; I never get high. Then from out of nowhere I find myself wondering, why not? What does it matter, anyway? And then I remember that night—it was almost a month ago now—when I saw Hugh throw the bronze rock at the barn door.

I'll bet you've never been drunk, he told me, *never gone skinny-dipping under a full moon, never filled a canvas with colors that take your breath away.*

What am I protecting myself from? I wonder. *What am I so afraid of?* If I can numb my mind, stop thinking—even for a few minutes—why shouldn't I?

I take the joint, inhale deeply. Of course I end up coughing like a fool and Trey cracks up, but I get control of myself and inhale again and again, until my throat burns and my head is spinning. Trey takes the tiny stub out of

41

my hand. The music is exploding, filling in the spaces around me like a watercolor wash.

"Don't think I didn't see that," Carly says, walking up, a sly smile on her face. "What brought on this sudden deterioration of moral fiber, Ms. Scully?"

"Nothing," I reply with a shrug. "Everything."

She laughs. "Well, go for it, my dear. Go for it."

We're dancing, all three of us now, and my feet feel as if they're six inches off the floor. There's a bottle in my hand and I'm gulping down the cool, sparkling liquid. My thoughts are free-form, floating; I can't focus on anything specific. There's just the music, the smoke, the peculiar tingling in my cheeks—and Trey, his yellow-green eyes scanning the room like radar, but always coming back to me.

Later, much later, I'm standing in the driveway outside Lori's house. The sky is black, no moon, and the stars seem to be rotating like searchlights. I reach in my purse, pull out my sketchbook. I'm trying to draw what I see, but all I can come up with is a page full of black scribbles. I turn the page and start again, but suddenly I'm listing to one side, then falling backward in slow motion. I feel strong hands around me, and I find myself looking up into Trey's laughing face.

"Come on," he says, "I'm going to drive you home."

"Since when do you have a license?"

"Since last month. I turned sixteen, remember?"

I don't, but that doesn't mean anything. I don't remember much right now. So I follow him to the car and get inside. He turns the key in the ignition, then pushes a tape into the cassette deck as he pulls out of the driveway.

Mill Road is deserted and R.E.M. is singing "So Fast, So Numb." I stare out the window at the lights in the passing houses. They seem so far away, so fleeting, and I feel I'm drifting, alone and apart, separate from the rest of the world. I don't know how to get back, how to connect. My house seems light-years away; Hugh and Marianna even farther.

Trey is talking, something about his call-back for the soap opera. He got the part, and his agent wants him to spend Christmas vacation in L.A., auditioning for film work.

"I don't know," he's saying. "I don't want to get marketed as some kind of brainless heartthrob. Maybe I should stay here, do some more theater in Princeton, maybe audition in New York." He glances at me. "Which driveway is yours?"

That's when I realize we're almost home. Marianna will be in bed, but Hugh will probably be in the studio. My stomach tightens as I see myself standing in the driveway, wanting to go inside but frightened of how Hugh will react if I do. Or the alternative—walking into a silent house, hearing Marianna call out to me as I pass her room. She'll take one look at me and know I'm wrecked.

A sick, panicky feeling shoots through me and I know I can't face either scenario. I turn to Trey and blurt out, "I don't want to go home."

He looks me over, curious, interested. "You don't?"

I'm thinking of Hugh again. Maybe I need to follow his advice, get out there and start living. Maybe that's what he wants, what he expects. Maybe that's what it's going to take to bring us together again. I turn to Trey, take a breath. "I want . . . I want to be with you."

He grins, then hits the accelerator and speeds past my driveway. I look at his profile, illuminated by the headlights of an oncoming car. His eyes are burning, intense.

He turns down a fire road and takes us bumping over rocks and mud puddles. Then he stops and turns off the engine, leaving the radio on. The music is so loud it makes the windows vibrate.

I turn to him, uncertain and anxious, a wisecrack on the

tip of my tongue. But before I can speak, his mouth is on mine, his weight presses me back against the door handle, his hands grope my breasts. My thoughts are fragments, disjointed images—a drumbeat, the red battery light on the dashboard, Trey's elbow jabbing into my ribs. He throws his leg over the gearshift, twists around, and now he's on my side, half-sitting, half-lying on top of me. I can hardly breathe as he rubs up against me, can hardly think as suddenly he shudders, groans, and stops moving.

For a long moment, nothing happens. Then he crawls awkwardly back to the driver's side and starts the car. The music pauses as he turns the key, then comes back louder than ever, filling the space between us, giving us an excuse not to speak.

And that's it. It's over. We never spoke a word, never looked into each other's eyes, never even took our clothes off, and we're bouncing up the fire road, on our way home.

Chapter 10

The next morning I wake up to the sound of rain pummeling my window. I close my eyes and go back to sleep, unable to face the day, unwilling to think about last night. It all feels like a dream anyway—why not keep on dreaming?

But my dreams turn to nightmares—Trey on top of me, crushing me, suffocating me; my father standing outside the car, peering through the window, laughing—and finally I force myself to get out of bed. I walk to the bathroom and gaze into the mirror. The girl staring back at me looks wasted, dark circles under her eyes, hair limp and smoky.

I step into the shower and let the scalding water wash away the grit, the smell of stale beer, the feel of Trey's lips on my skin. Then I dress and walk slowly down the hall, terrified of meeting Hugh, filled with the irrational certainty that he'll take one look at me and know what happened, know that what was supposed to be an exhilarating experience, a giant step into Hugh's no-holds-barred lifestyle turned out to be nothing but a pathetic teenage makeout session in the front seat of a car.

And why? Because I was too frightened, too self-conscious, too uptight. If I could have relaxed and responded, instead of cowering against the door like a startled doe, then maybe we could have found each other, could have given each other something—if not love, then pleasure, at least. A moment of joy.

The sound of Marianna's muffled voice pulls me back into the present. It's coming from my parents' bedroom. I pause outside the closed door, wishing I could walk in and tell her about last night. I long to feel her reach for my hand, to hear her comfort me, to reassure me, or even to scold me.

But the scenario is too foreign even to imagine. Instead, I lean closer to the door, hold my breath, and listen.

"You have to finish the new installation in time for the retrospective. The museum is promoting the show that way. And what about the critics, the collectors? They're all expecting to see a new work—something ground-breaking, something important."

"I can't do it, Marianna. I'm dizzy all the time, off balance. My hands won't do what I tell them to. I don't know what's happening to me."

"Yes, you do. It's a tumor, a small one—and it's getting smaller every day."

"Then why am I so weak?"

"Because you *think* you're weak. Don't you see what's happening, Hugh? You're letting yourself give in to the illness. You're letting it beat you."

He doesn't answer, so she continues.

"How do you want the art world to view this retrospective—as a summing up, an ending? This is what Hugh Scully created in his life, period? No. It's fine to take a look back at where you've come from, but at the same time, you want to show the world you're still in the game, still a force to be reckoned with."

"Am I? I don't know anymore. I don't—"

His voice fades away and she quickly fills the silence.

"I'm going to Houston tomorrow. There's a doctor down there who claims he's had excellent results with brain tumors. I've got an appointment to look at the clinic and learn about the treatments. According to the literature, it's only a month or two of intravenous injections—"

"And a few dozen enemas a week, I suppose." His voice is hard, bitter.

"Hugh, please. I know it's difficult to—"

"Who is this guy, anyway? Another quack like the one who came up with this useless diet you've got me on?"

"Keep your voice down. Do you want Sienna to hear you?"

"I don't care who hears me. I can't live like this. I'm miserable."

"Listen to me, Hugh," she says, her voice rising. "Traditional medicine hasn't done a thing to help you. Not a thing. So what do you want me to do? Give up? I won't do that. I *can't*."

"Okay, fine. Go to Houston. You can go to hell if you want to. Just leave me alone for five minutes. I want to rest."

There's a long moment of silence, then I hear Marianna's footsteps on the floor and I leap back into the bathroom just seconds before she opens the door. There's another silence, shorter this time, then she closes the door—carefully, quietly—and walks downstairs.

I spend the day in the woods behind the cornfields, hiking on a carpet of crackling brown leaves, wading through the frigid creek, sketching the crows as they scold me from their perch in the half-bare trees. Daylight savings ended days ago, but I'm not yet accustomed to the early darkness. When the sun falls below the trees, I'm far from home, stomach growling, fingertips numb, calf muscles sore.

I stumble through the underbrush, half hoping I'm going in the wrong direction, half wishing I didn't have to go home. Tonight the uneven ground, the brambles, the deepening shadows seem more welcoming than the old farmhouse, more comforting than the faces of my mother and father. Yet somehow my internal compass leads me back to the cornfield, and soon I'm tramping out the other side, heading around the back of the barn.

Hugh is in the studio; I can see the light under the doors, hear the dissonant wail of a Schönberg string quartet. I don't even think of going inside, and barely pause as I walk to the house. A note on the kitchen counter tells me that Liesel has left a bowl of lamb stew in the refrigerator for me. I heat it in the microwave and head upstairs.

On the top step I freeze, cock my head. A strange gulping sound, muffled and mysterious, is coming from the bathroom. I wait, confused and uncertain. And then the gulping changes to a sort of high-pitched mewing, like the moan of an injured cat, and all at once I realize that I know that voice, know what's happening. It's Marianna, it's my mother, and she's crying.

A sick, unsteady feeling surges through me and suddenly I'm standing on a precarious, rocky ledge looking down, down into blackness, about to fall. And I allow myself to consider—can no longer *not* consider—the possibility that perhaps Marianna doesn't have all the answers, can't solve every problem, isn't as strong and sure and certain as she pretends to be. That maybe she's just as worried, just as bewildered, just as terrified as I am.

The thought chills me, sends me running to my room with a panicked sob rising up in my throat. Because if Marianna isn't in control, isn't taking care of things, isn't guiding Hugh on a straight course from sickness back to health, then anything is possible—time could stand still, the earth could collide with the sun, and Hugh Scully, my father, could die.

Chapter 11

The next morning, Marianna appears at breakfast looking serene and rested, and I find myself wondering if I was hallucinating last night. Maybe I was projecting my own fears onto her, my own uncertainties. I want to believe it, want to convince myself that it was *my* weakness, not hers, that sent me running to my room, kept me huddled in my bed, my back against the cold wall, sobbing silently in the dark.

As I leave for school, she kisses me on the forehead. "I'm going back to L.A.," she says. "The first pieces of Hugh's new installation are being shipped out and I want to be there to help unpack them."

I don't let on that I know she's lying. I don't want to know. So I place the truth in a little box and add it to the stack inside my head. It's getting harder to keep the boxes in order, but that just makes the job all the more important. I force myself to nod and smile. *Everything is going to be all right*, I tell myself, repeating the words like a mantra. *Everything is going to be just fine.*

And for a while, it is. I'm petrified of seeing Trey at school, certain he's told everyone what happened after Lori's party, convinced he's expecting it to happen again. But our first encounter—before homeroom on the lawn in front of the library—turns out to be nothing. Less than nothing. He smiles and starts talking about homework. Then Carly walks up and he launches into a long story about some actress he met at an audition in New York. It's almost as if the whole fiasco on the fire road never happened, and I don't know whether to feel insulted or relieved. So I take the easy way out. I don't allow myself to feel anything at all.

A day or two later, Hugh's health begins to improve. When I come home from school on Wednesday, he's in his studio, using the spray gun. His back is to me as I walk by and I can see the muscles on his upper arms flexing as he bends over, spraying lacquer on the bronze object at his feet.

"Have you noticed?" Liesel whispers when she brings dinner up to my room the next evening. "Your father is standing straighter. He isn't dragging his leg."

It's true. I'm in the kitchen later that evening when he walks in the side door. His shoulders are straight and even. It even seems he's putting on weight.

Marianna's right, I tell myself. *He's getting better.* I'm so happy I don't even care that he hasn't paid any attention to me since Marianna left, hasn't called me into his studio or asked me to eat with him, barely nods as he strides through the kitchen and heads into the living room. *If he gets well*, I think, *that's all that matters. I won't ask for more.*

It's Friday evening, almost a week since Marianna left. I'm in my room, sketching the black walnut tree, a leafless skeleton silhouetted against the autumn sky. There's a knock at the door. It's Liesel, but without my dinner.

"Do you want to eat downstairs?" she asks. "Mr. Scully went out early this morning and he told me he won't be back until late."

"Where did he go?"

"Philadelphia. I drove him to the train."

So I eat downstairs, channel surfing in front of the TV. I get hooked on a foreign movie and stay downstairs longer than I planned, then go back up to my room to read and sketch. It's after midnight when I hear a knock at my door. I open it, figuring it must be Liesel but unable to imagine what she could possibly want at this hour.

Instead, Hugh is standing there. His cheeks are flushed, his hair is windblown. He's still wearing his coat, carrying a black leather portfolio under his arm.

"Can I come in?" he asks. He's looking past me, his eyes scanning the room.

I don't answer right away. I'm too stunned, too bewildered. Hugh never seeks me out, never comes to my room. "Sure," I say at last. "Come in."

He tosses the portfolio on the floor and takes a seat on the edge of my bed. I sit stiffly on my desk chair, unable to imagine why he's come. He gazes at the floor, at the hooked rug, at the chair leg. Then he speaks, so softly I have to lean forward to hear. "The tumor is malignant."

The words don't make sense. They sound like gibberish. "What?"

"It's the size of an orange. I thought it was benign. I let Marianna convince me it was. But it's not. It's malignant and it's growing."

"No," I say automatically. "It's getting smaller. Marianna said so."

"So did the doctor. But I went to another doctor, one who doesn't know me, doesn't know Marianna. He did a whole battery of tests." He motions toward the portfolio. "I have the results."

Panic is rising in my chest, but I force myself to breathe deeply, to push it back down. "You can have an operation," I say. "They can cut it out."

He shakes his head. "It's like a weed. They can cut off the stem, but they can't get at the root. It's too deep, too tangled up with the rest of my brain. And unless the root is removed, the stem will just grow back."

"I don't believe it," I insist. "The doctor's wrong. *You're* wrong."

He smiles, a sad, lopsided smile. "I'm dying, Sienna. I've got a few more months, maybe a year at the most."

The panic is pushing up through my throat, making me want to scream. I've got to fight it. I jump up, kick my father's portfolio across the floor. "You're lying! I know you're lying!"

He doesn't react, just looks up at me and says, "I want to go to the island. I want you to come with me."

I'm so distraught, it takes me a second to figure out what he's talking about. Then memories of our island, Birch Cove Island, flash through my head. I see the cabin, the little shack behind it that Hugh uses for a studio. I feel cold ocean waves lapping against my shins. I breathe in damp New England fog, taste wild blueberries on my tongue.

The images distract me, soothe me, and the panic subsides a little. And then the reality of what he's saying hits me. "Come with you? Me?" I say.

"I don't trust myself to drive alone," Hugh replies. "I get dizzy, and since I stopped the medication I've been having seizures again."

For an instant I had allowed myself to imagine he wanted my company, wanted *me*, but even knowing the truth pleases me. I want to help him, would do anything for him. But I only have a learner's permit; I'm barely halfway through driver's ed.

"What if I get in an accident?" I ask. "What if—?"

"You'll be fine. It's only an eight or nine hour drive to Teal Harbor. Between the two of us, we can handle it."

"But what about Marianna? I thought she was due back Monday night."

"We'll be home before then. I just need to get away for a day or two. I need to think."

The way he talks, it sounds as if Marianna knows everything, as if she suggested the trip to the island herself. Or is that just what I want to believe? I rub my palms across my jeans. I don't want to know.

"We're going to leave now," he continues. "Tonight."

"Tonight? But—"

"Tonight." His features are relaxed, but there's a look of determination in his eyes, of desperation. When he speaks again, his voice is hoarse, urgent. "Pack your things and meet me in the driveway. Do you hear me, Sienna? Do it now."

He doesn't wait for a response. Just stands up, grabs the portfolio, and walks quickly out the door.

I'm standing over an unzipped canvas duffel bag, staring blankly at the two sweatshirts in my hands, unable to choose between them, unable to focus, to think. My head is spinning with questions. My hands are trembling.

"My father is dying," I whisper, trying out the sounds, the sense of it. But I still don't believe it. It must be a mistake, I tell myself, some foul-up by the doctor or the lab technicians.

But what if it *is* true? What if Marianna was lying about Hugh's condition? Or what if she simply didn't know the truth?

I drop the sweatshirts and head for the door, determined to find Liesel and ask her where my mother is staying in

Houston. I'm going to call and find out what's going on. I can almost hear her voice, so calm, so reassuring. "Everything is just fine, Sienna. Now put Hugh on the phone. I'm going to take care of this."

But before my fingers even touch the doorknob, I've changed my mind. She doesn't know Hugh's been to a new doctor, I'm sure of it. She doesn't know he's leaving for Maine in the middle of the night, that he's taking me along. If I call her, she'll catch the first plane home and put a stop to everything. She'll tell Hugh he isn't strong enough to handle a trip to the island. She'll send him back into the studio, tell him he has to stay focused on his work, his goals.

I know immediately I can't let that happen. Hugh has taken me into his confidence. He's trusting me to help him, and I can't let him down. Because if my father is dying—if it's even a remote possibility—then his last months should be his own. If he wants to go to the island—*needs* to go—who am I to deny his wishes? How can I—or anyone—say no?

But there's something else that's stopping me from calling Marianna. If she comes back now and takes over, I'll be on the outside again, invisible and alone. But if I can find the courage to pack my bag, to get in the car and go, then I'll have a chance—maybe my last chance—to spend time with Hugh. To make him notice me. To really connect.

I walk back to the bed, shove both sweatshirts into the duffel bag, and zip it up. Then I hoist the bag over my shoulder and hurry downstairs to join my father.

PART II

The Road

Chapter 12

Hugh is already in the Range Rover, lights off, engine idling. I tiptoe across the gravel, feeling like a criminal. It's a scary feeling, but exciting, too, and I'm breathless, filled with butterflies as I slip into the passenger seat and toss my duffel bag into the back.

Hugh doesn't look at me, just puts the car in gear and backs slowly down the driveway. The whole thing feels unreal, like a movie, the camera pulling back to take in the barn, the farmhouse, the trees. I lean forward in my seat and peer up at the third floor, at Liesel's room, half expecting to see her standing at the window, watching us. But her lights are off; in fact, the whole house is dark and getting smaller, receding as we cruise slowly backward.

Then the driveway snakes left through black trees and we're pulling out into the road. Hugh turns on the headlights, hits the accelerator, then reaches over and pops a tape into the cassette deck. Instantly, the car is filled with the sounds of Anita O'Day crooning a swinging version of "Sweet Georgia Brown" at some long-ago jazz concert.

I flash back to the fire road, to R.E.M. blasting through the speakers, to Trey groping me across the gear shift. I was looking for a new truth that night, a revelation, but I didn't find it. Now I'm running off in the middle of the night with my father, searching for another way to free myself, a better way. But Hugh is looking straight ahead, tapping his fingers against the steering wheel, more aware of the music than of me.

I lean my head against the window, wondering why I've come. Hugh's acting normal, driving fine. He doesn't need me. I tell myself I should have stayed home, promised him I'd play dumb about his disappearance, and gone to bed. But when I imagine the weekend, the long days hiking on trails I've traveled a hundred times before, the silent evenings eating in front of the television, doing homework in my room, I know why I'm here. Because this trip is a possibility, a question mark, *something*. And something—even this—is better than nothing.

Hugh drives over the bridge into New Jersey, takes 202 toward Flemington. I've driven this route every summer of my life, but I never paid much attention to it. Now I may have to drive it myself. I study the white line, mentally moving the steering wheel to parallel it, feeling incompetent and unprepared.

The music pauses, the cassette deck switches to the other side of the tape. "Are you okay?" I blurt into the silence.

Hugh hits the eject button, turns to me. "What?"

"Can you drive? Are you all right?"

He nods. "I feel pretty good right now. Maybe because I'm finally doing something."

It almost sounds as if Hugh feels the same way I do. But how can he? What he was doing in his studio wasn't nothing. "What about the new installation?" I ask. "How's it going?"

He taps the steering wheel, ignoring my question. "I'd kill for a pastrami sandwich."

"But your diet? Marianna said—"

"Marianna says a lot of things."

"She's trying to help you."

"I know. That's all she's ever tried to do."

He pushes the cassette back in and Anita O'Day is singing again, something about "Miss Otis Regrets." Regrets what? I try to listen, but my mind keeps drifting up the road to the Maine coast, to Birch Cove Island.

I don't have to ask why Hugh wants to go there. Each year, when there are still patches of snow on the ground, when the only signs of spring are a warm breeze and a few trembling crocuses pushing through the damp earth, he begins talking about Birch Cove, begins making plans to leave. I think he'd live there if he could build a real studio, a foundry. But there's no electricity on the island, no heat. We use kerosene lanterns and cook over a wood-burning stove.

Hugh turns down the music, glances at me. He's thinking about the island, too. "It's going to be cold up there," he says.

I nod. "We've never been on the island this late in the year."

"Marianna spent Christmas there once," he says. "Back when she was a kid."

"Marianna went to the island when she was little?" I ask uncertainly. "But I thought you bought the island together, before I was born."

"No, it's been in her family for years." He chuckles. "Maybe that's why she hates it so much. The place comes with a lot of emotional baggage."

I'm too stunned to speak. I didn't know Marianna spent part of her childhood there or that she hated the place. But now that I think about it, I remember that every year she delays going up as long as possible, finds reasons why we need to stay in New Hope or travel to Manhattan for art openings, parties, meetings. Once we're there, she returns home often, always taking me with her, claiming that Hugh needs to think, to work, to be alone.

"And now . . . and now the island belongs to her?"

He nods. "Her parents left it to her. She didn't tell me about it until we'd been married almost a year. I think she knew I'd love it. But you can't build a serious art career living on a lump of sand in the middle of Mussel Bay. She understood that, and she made me understand it, too."

"You lived in New York then?"

"In the Village. Then you came along. I was getting into sculpture by then anyway and I needed a bigger studio. So Marianna closed her gallery and I signed on with Evelyn Fadulo. Then we bought the farmhouse."

I hesitate. My parents rarely talk about the past, never volunteer information on their own, so I've never felt encouraged to ask questions. But tonight feels different. The look in Hugh's eyes is distant, wistful. He might tell me more, if only I don't break the spell. "You lived in Boston before you moved to Manhattan, didn't you?" I ask softly. I read it in a book once, a survey of his work.

"I grew up there. After college, I got a gig teaching art at a junior college out in the 'burbs. Mostly, I was painting—and sweet-talking my female students into bed." He chuckles, remembering. "Back then, I had a romantic view of the artistic life. I saw myself living in an attic, painting in obscurity until I died—young, of course—and my genius was discovered."

I stare at him, stunned. It's not the sex part that throws me, not really. It's the idea that he was once an unknown painter, teaching at a tiny junior college, far away from the galleries and museums of New York.

"I'd still be there if it wasn't for Marianna," he says. "Back then she managed a little gallery in the Village. We met at a party in Boston and the next day she showed up at the college asking to see my work. I guess she saw some-thing in it—some tiny spark of potential talent—because she took one of the paintings to put in the gallery's next show."

I wait for Hugh to go on, but he pops in the tape again and turns up the volume. I try to picture my father as a young painter, full of raw talent and romantic notions. Even then Marianna knew what he was capable of, what he needed.

The thought worries me because tonight Hugh isn't pay-ing attention to what Marianna thinks he needs. He's run-ning away, like a kid with his belongings tied in a handkerchief on the end of a stick. And I'm along for the ride. I've even promised to help him.

A glowing green sign appears in front of us, floating in the darkness. Route 78, it says. Newark and New York City. Hugh swerves into the right lane, takes the exit. This isn't the way to Maine, I know it.

"Where are you going?" I shout over the music.

"I need to talk to Evelyn Fadulo," he shouts back. "I need a pastrami sandwich."

"Tonight?" I ask. "But I thought we were driving straight up to Teal Harbor."

Hugh doesn't answer. He just merges onto the highway, slides over into the left lane, and goes.

Chapter 13

After the dark emptiness of rural New Jersey, Manhattan is a carnival ride with careening taxis, blaring horns, music, and voices. Traffic lights flash red, yellow, green, and even now, at one-thirty in the morning, there are people, so many people.

Hugh cruises up East Eighty-ninth, then circles the block a half-dozen times before squeezing into a microspace vacated by a police car. He gets out and I follow, wondering where we're going and why we're here.

"It's kind of late," I say. "Maybe we should wait until tomorrow to visit."

"Evelyn never goes to bed before two or three," he replies, grabbing the bags and shutting the door with his hip. "She'll be up."

I've been to Evelyn Fadulo's gallery five, maybe six times when Hugh was having a show, but I have no idea where she lives. It's hard to imagine her away from the gallery, as a real person with a home and a life. I picture her long face, copper-colored skin, shiny black hair falling across her cheeks as she leans down to pour a glass of wine. If we've ever made eye contact, I can't remember it.

Hugh strides down the sidewalk, then heads up the steps of a three-story brownstone and rings the bell. The door opens and Evelyn is standing there in a pale blue caftan, her hair piled casually on her head, long silver earrings dangling against her cheeks.

"Hugh! What are you doing here?" Even in her startled state, her voice is soft, melodic. There's a stillness about her, a sort of serenity that envelops her like a second skin.

"Am I interrupting anything?" Hugh asks.

"Of course not." She turns to me. "Heavens, you must be Sienna. Last time I saw you, you were six inches shorter." She turns back to Hugh, frowning, uncertain. "Is everything all right?"

"Sure it is. I just had to get some perspective on this new piece I'm working on, that's all. We're heading up to the Adirondacks for a few days."

"At this time of year?"

Hugh doesn't answer, just looks past her into the house, and now I know for certain that this trip is a secret. From Marianna. From everyone. "You want to go to the Carnegie Deli?" he asks. "I'm starving."

"Don't be silly. I've got plenty of food here. Come inside."

Hugh walks in like he knows his way around. The room is warm and stylish, with cream-colored sofas, a large Oriental rug, and walls full of contemporary art. I recognize a Jim Dine, a David Hockney, plus one of Hugh's early bronze pieces, a chair with a shirt draped over the back and a wallet and keys on the seat.

Hugh drops the bags beside one of the sofas and keeps walking. I follow, too timid to take off my jacket, and find myself in a dining room with a low, black lacquered table surrounded by pastel-colored silk cushions. I picture him here with Marianna, discussing art, planning his career. He kicks off his shoes and stretches out, comfortable, at home.

"Where's Marianna?" Evelyn asks, echoing my thoughts.

"In Houston. She's got a friend down there. Her best friend from college."

I look at him, startled to realize that Evelyn doesn't know about the tumor, that Hugh doesn't want her to know.

Evelyn goes into the kitchen and returns with brie, fruit, bread, and wine. She sits, then looks at me, still standing in the doorway, and pats the cushion beside her. "Come in, Sienna. Make yourself comfortable."

I slip off my shoes and sit awkwardly at the table, trying to look as if sharing a midnight snack with my father and his dealer is something I do all the time. But I don't know where to put my feet, don't know what to say, or even what expression to wear.

If Evelyn notices, she doesn't let on. She pours wine for all three of us, then holds up her glass and smiles. "To the L.A. retrospective," she says.

"To the past," Hugh replies.

"And the future."

He chuckles softly. "We all know where *that* leads. An obituary in the *Times*, and then the price of my work will skyrocket. You'll be rich—well, richer—and Sienna will have college all paid for."

Evelyn looks startled, then recovers and laughs. "You're awful, Hugh." We clink glasses and sip the wine. She offers me a plate of fruit. "Have you thought about college, Sienna?"

"Not really." I take a slice of apple and bite into it. The taste is tart and sweet, and I hold it under my tongue like a secret. The secret Hugh and I share.

"Perhaps you'd like to follow in your father's footsteps," Evelyn suggests.

I shake my head. "I'm no artist."

"Marianna says she's got some talent," Hugh says. "I don't know. She won't let me look in her precious sketchbooks."

"Then she *must* be an artist. She keeps her work private until she's sure it's ready. Like you, Mr. Scully. When are you going to let me come down to the farmhouse and see what you're working on?"

"When it's finished. *If* it's ever finished."

"What are you talking about? That piece is promised to the retrospective. After that, it goes straight into my gallery."

He doesn't answer. Just slathers some brie on a piece of bread, puts the whole thing in his mouth, and chews. It's his first time off the diet and he looks stoned from the intensity of the flavors. He gulps the wine, reaches for some more bread.

"How long can you stay, Hugh?" Evelyn asks. "I'm holding an opening tomorrow evening that I think you'd be interested in. A young woman, Gillian Ferris. It's clear she's been influenced by you."

"Tell me more. What's her work like?"

"Interesting. Carved wooden interiors, very realistic, but then defaced—the surfaces have been cut and scratched, some are spray-painted with graffiti."

"I've often thought of doing that to my work, then tossing it in the garbage," Hugh says. I think about the night I saw him hurl the bronze rock against the door of the studio. It was as if he loathed the sight of it, as if he was trying to fling it into orbit, into outer space.

But Evelyn interprets Hugh's remark as a sarcastic comment on Gillian Ferris's art. "Don't be catty," she scolds. "Her work has been very well-received. I think you should see it."

"Am I supposed to be worried?" Hugh asks irritably.

"I just want you to be aware of her. Her pieces are

getting bigger. I think she's moving in the direction of large-scale environments."

"And I'm moving away. Far away."

"What?" Evelyn looks worried. "What are you working on, Hugh? If you're moving in a new direction, I think I have a right to know."

"I told you. I'm not working. I'm on vacation." He finishes his wine, then reaches for the bottle and pours some more. "I feel like getting smashed."

A faint smile plays on her lips. "Go right ahead."

I watch them sip their wine and I'm filled with a sadness that makes my chest ache. We're only two hours from home and already I'm on the outside again, trying to interpret my father's tone of voice, his body language, trying to make him notice me.

I feel Evelyn's eyes on me and I look up. "You seem tired, Sienna. Would you like to go to bed?"

I glance over at Hugh. "I thought you wanted to drive straight through."

"What does it matter?" he says. "We'll get there when we get there."

Evelyn stands and I obediently follow. She leads me upstairs to a guest room with royal blue walls and white linens on the bed. "The bathroom is across the hall," she says. "There are towels in the closet."

Then she's gone and I'm alone. I look around and my eyes are drawn to a large, abstract painting on the wall above the bed. It's the colors I notice first—a beautiful eggplant purple, midnight blue, indigo, and gold. Next, the shapes—graceful ovals, sweeping spirals, and a thin, serpentine line that weaves its way between the shapes, binding them all together.

It isn't until I step closer that I realize there are shapes beneath the shapes, dark colors coated with a thin layer of lighter pigment, delicate strokes over thick slabs of paint.

And I'm drawn into the canvas, going deeper and deeper, exploring each layer, each color, each line.

I step back to take in the whole, then crawl onto the bed to search for a name at the bottom of the painting. My breath catches in my throat when I find it.

H. Scully. My father.

I step back and stare, consumed by what I'm seeing. I haven't looked at one of his oil paintings since I was a little kid, and I don't remember what I once saw. Even the biographical books I've read include only one or two paintings, reproduced in black and white. And I find myself wondering why Hugh stopped painting, why he turned his back on color and line and chose instead to pour bronze.

A warm tear grazes my upper lip and that's when I realize I'm crying. Crying for what I don't know about my father, for what I'll never know. Because he's dying, and there's nothing I can do about it.

I press my tongue hard against the roof of my mouth, fighting to stay in control. And suddenly I know there's only one way to calm myself, to shut down my brain and put my emotions on hold. I have to pick up a pencil and draw something.

My duffel bag, with my sketchbook and drawing pencils inside, is still in the living room. So I go into the bathroom and throw water on my face, then tiptoe down the stairs, hoping maybe Hugh and Evelyn are in the kitchen and I can slip in and out without them noticing.

There's no sound from the first floor, just silence, so I take another step, then another, until I reach the bottom stair. Then I hear it—a sigh, a quiet moan. And see it— Hugh and Evelyn standing together at the head of the table, her head tipped back, black hair falling loose, his hand around her waist, their lips together.

Chapter 14

I don't move, don't breathe. I feel enormous, so obvious, but they don't see me, don't even realize I'm there. So I take one step backward, moving in reverse, trying to rewind myself into the past. It's then that the stair creaks and they look up, mouths moist, eyes wide.

"Sienna," Hugh breathes.

I run past them, out the front door and down the brownstone steps. I don't know where I'm going; I just have to get out of there. But Hugh catches up to me before my shoes touch the sidewalk. He grabs my arm, turns me toward him. "Sienna, that wasn't what it looked like."

"It wasn't?" I respond, eager to be convinced, to accept it as a trick of light, a hallucination, anything but what it seemed.

"It was just—I don't know—an impulse."

I should let it go at that, but I need more. So I blurt out the most extreme thing I can think of, praying he'll deny it. "Are you . . . are you having an affair with her?"

He frowns, drops my arm, and turns away. "Stop, Sienna. It was nothing. Forget about it, okay?"

"Forget about it?" I repeat, trying to understand, trying desperately to cram what I saw into one of the little boxes inside my head. "Is that what you want me to do?"

He spins around, eyes flashing. "You heard me, Sienna!" he growls. "Just drop it. This doesn't concern you."

His sudden anger is like a slap, and I take a step backward, stumbling against the handrail. I feel exhausted, numb, and my eyes are full of tears.

Hugh stares at me. "Sienna, for God's sake, don't you get it? I'm dying."

His words scare me so much I can barely breathe. "Maybe Marianna's right," I whisper. "Maybe that doctor in Houston can help you."

He shakes his head. "I can't listen to Marianna anymore. She's always been there, telling me what to do, what to think, what to feel. I've got to do this on my own."

"Do what?"

"I don't know. Something that matters. Not to Marianna or anyone else, but to me." He drops his hands, then starts up the steps to Evelyn's front door. "It's late, Sienna," he mutters. "Let's go to bed."

I just stand there, too shell-shocked to think, even to move. So he comes back, puts his arm around my shoulder, and we walk up the stairs side by side, together.

I'm lying in the white bed, gazing at Hugh's painting in the darkness, and I can't sleep. My body feels heavy, immobile, but my mind is racing. I keep seeing Evelyn and my father together, their lips touching, their bodies entwined. And then I hear Hugh telling me he's dying, that he wants to do something that matters, and I try to reconcile that with the Hugh Scully I know, or think I know.

I see him lifting a crucible of molten bronze, his powerful arms tensed, his eyes alive with the joy of creation, as a crowd of onlookers lean forward, amazed, intent. Or eating dinner with Marianna, their voices rising and falling in a kind of intimate dance, their eyes locked on each other, only each other. How can that man, that Hugh Scully, think his life hasn't mattered?

Then I remember that night in the studio, the night he caught me watching him. "Why don't you and Marianna just leave me alone?" he shouted. As if it wasn't only me he wanted to be rid of, but her as well. Or tonight, when he told me he wanted to do something that mattered. "Not to Marianna or anyone else," he said, "but to me."

And suddenly I'm creating a mental portrait of my mother that's subtly changed, with different highlights, different shadings. It's a portrait of a woman who uses her influence not only to encourage and inspire, to protect and comfort, but also to manipulate, to control.

I sit up and hug my knees beneath the comforter, remembering how she lied to Hugh about his illness, how she told him the tumor was small and getting smaller all the time. I remember the way she pressured him to return to his studio after the radiation treatments, kept him working even when his head was pounding, when his hands were too unsteady to hold a welding torch.

What really matters to Marianna? I ask myself. Is it Hugh's well-being, his happiness? Or is it his success she craves? His money and his fame?

At that moment, with darkness all around me and my mother many miles away, I can almost convince myself that what Hugh did isn't so terrible, or even so surprising. He's sick, I tell myself, he's frightened and confused. Who can blame him for wanting to escape from Marianna's demands, at least for a moment, for giving in to the temptation to lose himself in Evelyn's arms?

The thought calms me, comforts me, and I wrap it around me like a shawl. I wrap the white comforter around me, too, tucking it under my feet and pulling it up to my chin. Then I close my eyes and forgive.

Chapter 15

When I open my eyes the next morning, Hugh is standing over me. "What time is it?" I ask, blinking back the sunlight.

"Almost eleven. I'm going to the Museum of Modern Art. Do you want to come?"

I nod and I roll out of bed, certain I must be sleepwalking. This is all I've wanted my entire life—for Hugh to notice me, to want to be with me. I feel like hugging him, but I don't know how he'll react. So I just stand there, watching him leave.

I jump in the shower, then throw on my clothes and hurry downstairs. Hugh is in the kitchen, sipping coffee. Evelyn is nowhere in sight.

"Ready?" he asks.

I nod and grab a croissant from the counter. My duffel bag is still in the living room. I take out my sketchbook and pencils, stuff them into my backpack, and follow Hugh outside. It's the beginning of November and it feels like it. The wind surges down the streets, creating minicyclones of litter and dust, blowing my hair across my eyes. Hugh turns up his collar and heads for Fifth Avenue, limping slightly but moving fast, not talking.

The sidewalks are crowded with Saturday shoppers, tourists, kids from the suburbs. We hail a cab and Hugh leans forward in the seat, hands gripping his knees, eyes fixed on the street ahead. His tension is catching and I find myself clenching my jaw, silently urging the driver to pass that bus, slide through that yellow light, go faster, *faster*.

When we walk into the museum, everything changes. Hugh's smiling now, strolling through the lobby, breathing the air like a bouquet. I walk beside him, trying to look like I know my way around although I've never been here before. Except for a couple of school trips to the Philadelphia Museum of Art, I haven't been to any art museums at all.

Hugh quickens his stride and I hurry after him. We're in the galleries now, and all around me are paintings I've seen a hundred times in books, only in real life they're bigger, brighter, more dazzling than a thousand exploding stars.

"Look at that red," Hugh says, stopping in front of a huge Rothko. "I can feel it in here." He thumps his chest. "Damn, I can taste it."

I imagine myself embracing the color, squeezing it tight, and now it's inside me, too, burning, blazing. I turn away and find myself drawn toward a painting by Franz Kline, a white background filled with thick slashes of black that seem to cut through me, dissecting the red, blotting it out.

Hugh sees it an instant later and we stop, paralyzed by its intensity and power. Then he takes my arm and leads me through the rooms to Mondrian's *Broadway Boogie Woogie*. "How did he do that?" he asks in hushed tones. "He

73

uses static squares to create movement; three primary hues to imply a kaleidoscope of color."

I'm still trying to figure it out as Hugh heads down the hallway that overlooks the sculpture garden. I follow him, then pause at the window, certain he'll want to point out his favorite sculptures, that he'll insist on taking me out there so I can get close to them. But he doesn't slow down, doesn't even glance out the window, just keeps walking until we're in another gallery, standing in front of a wall of Kandinskys.

I take one look and catch my breath because every color, every texture, every line makes sense, perfect sense. The effect is so intense, so exciting, that I feel elated, almost giddy. My skin is tingling and my knees are weak.

" 'Why should we not succeed in creating color harmonies that correspond to our psychic state?' " Hugh asks softly.

"What?"

"Gauguin asked the question and Kandinsky answered it. He painted what he felt in his heart. It was completely independent of physical reality. It was visual music."

I think about the canvas hanging in Evelyn's guest room—the layered shapes, the vibrant colors. "You used to paint like that," I say.

Hugh barks a laugh. "Not even close. Anyway, why kill myself trying to do something that's already been done better?"

"But your paintings were wonderful," I insist. "Besides, if it's what you love—"

"Let me give you a piece of advice, Sienna," he says with a smirk. "If you want to succeed in today's market, doing what you love isn't going to cut it. What's important is to create something that will catch the public's attention. Something quirky or funny maybe, or just huge and labor-intensive. People are impressed by that sort of thing."

I think about his installations—their scope, their size, the many months it takes to create one. "Is . . . is that why you switched to sculpture?" I ask in disbelief.

He doesn't answer, just gazes at the Kandinskys. Then he takes my arm, leads me back through time, past works by Picasso, Matisse, Cezanne, and Van Gogh, until my brain is exploding with colors, with images, and I feel humbled, intimidated. But despite my fears, my fingers are itching to pick up a pencil, a crayon—*anything*—and draw everything I see, everything I've ever seen, everything I feel.

"Come on," Hugh says, as we walk out into the hubbub of Fifty-third Street. "I'm going to buy you the best pastrami sandwich you ever tasted."

We descend into the subway and when we come up again we're downtown, in the Village. "Marianna and I lived over there," he tells me, motioning across Washington Square, "in a fourth floor walk-up. I used to go up on the roof and sketch the park at sunrise, then again at sunset."

He leads me over to Lafayette Street, to a storefront deli with salamis hanging in the window. I sit across from him in a booth with red plastic benches, not quite knowing where to look, where to put my hands. This is not something we ever do together, not something that comes naturally to me, and when the waitress brings my menu I bury my head in it, happy to have an excuse not to talk.

It isn't until the sandwiches arrive and the smell of warm pastrami fills my nostrils that I realize how hungry I am. I take a huge bite and Hugh looks at me expectantly. "Mmmm," I mumble.

He laughs, delighted, then takes a bite of his own sandwich. "I don't care if Marianna is right about that damned diet," he says. "This pastrami is worth dying for."

It's the only joke I've heard him make about his illness, the first even vaguely humorous thing either of us has said on this trip, and we both laugh loudly, too loudly. Still, it feels good, like standing up and stretching after a long day in school, and I can feel us both relaxing, settling down, and starting to feel comfortable with each other.

"It must have been so exciting to live here," I say wistfully. "Everything was happening for you—you were in love, your career was taking off . . ."

He takes a sip of his coffee and frowns into the cup. "My career wasn't taking off. My piece in the group show never got mentioned in the reviews. The first solo show didn't happen until six months later, and the response was only lukewarm."

"You weren't working in bronze then?"

"I was painting, only painting, and God, it was hard. Every day, every minute, every brush stroke was a struggle. I wanted to make something no one had ever seen before. Something that would move people, that would take their breath away. Then one day Marianna suggested I try my hand at sculpture."

"But why?"

He shakes his head, runs a hand through his hair. "Maybe she knew something I didn't—about me, about the market. I don't know. As far as I was concerned, it was just an escape, a break from the rigors of painting. Eventually, though, I got interested in bronze casting, and I grew to love the process. It's so physical, so concrete."

"But why did you give up painting?"

"I didn't at first. But then Marianna put some of my bronzes in the gallery, and they sold." He laughs softly. "I couldn't believe it. Compared to painting, pouring bronze was so easy for me. So I did some more pieces, each one a little bigger, a little more complex."

I frown. "Because it was easy?"

He looks up, meets my eye. "Because it was a relief to finally be turning out something that people liked, that made money. Something that didn't take my entire heart and soul to create."

I stare at him, dumbfounded. "But if it doesn't take your heart and soul, what's the point?"

"What's the point of those doodles you're always making in your sketchbooks, Sienna?" he asks pointedly. "Are they about heart and soul? Do they consume your thoughts and overwhelm your senses? Are they your passion, your reason for being alive?"

I think about the dozens and dozens of sketchbooks stacked neatly on the shelves of my room, each filled with careful pencil drawings of plants, of furniture, of rocks and dishes and weathervanes and birds. They're like the boxes inside my head—orderly and contained, and I realize they have nothing to do with heart and soul, with passion. They're about escape. They're about survival.

I look away, my cheeks burning. "I'm not an artist," I insist, emphasizing the *I*, trying to turn the focus back on him. "I never claimed to be."

"You could be," he says, leaning across the table, reaching out his hand to lift my chin until we're gazing into each other's eyes. "If you opened yourself up to the world around you. If you let yourself live."

I remember the feel of Trey's body rubbing against mine, the sound of his breath in my ear. I tried opening up, and it was a disaster.

I push his hand away. "I've seen your idea of living," I say bitterly. "Gulping down a bottle of wine and feeling up Evelyn Fadulo. Sorry, Hugh, I'm not impressed."

"Sienna, don't," he says, shaking his head. "I didn't mean for you to see that. I didn't mean . . . "

His voice trails off and there's a sadness in his eyes I've never seen before. *Does he expect me to forgive him?* I wonder. But it isn't the kiss I can't forgive. It's finding out that the bronze pieces I thought meant so much to him aren't the result of burning passion. He didn't even come to them on his own. They're just a cop-out, elegant hunks of metal designed to impress the public and make a buck.

Chapter 16

Hugh pays for the sandwiches, dropping his wallet in the process. "Damn," he mutters, reaching down to retrieve it. When he comes back up, he leans his elbows against the table and holds his head.

"What's wrong?" I ask.

"The room is spinning." He lifts his left hand and tries to make a fist, but his fingers will only close partway. "My whole left side feels weak. God, I'm a mess."

"No, you're not," I insist, but I'm lying. Hugh has always seemed larger than life to me, like a portrait painted in bold strokes and vivid colors. But now, as he sits across from me, fumbling with his wallet, it's the little things I notice—the dark circles under his eyes, the red scar on his hand where he burned himself with the welding torch, the way his collar hangs a little too loose around his neck.

"Let's go," he says, standing up.

"Where?"

"To Gillian Ferris's opening."

We leave the restaurant and start walking, back to Washington Square and then up Fifth Avenue. The sun is going down and the wind is fierce. Taxis are everywhere, but Hugh doesn't stop to hail one, doesn't seem to notice.

"I tried to go back to painting a couple of times," he says suddenly.

I walk faster, straining to hear him over the wind and the traffic.

"Marianna said it was a mistake," he continues. "I was making a name for myself as a sculptor. If I changed direction again, the critics would lose interest."

"Maybe she was wrong," I tell him.

"She was right. Marianna understood the New York art scene. And Evelyn agreed with her."

"But why did you have to listen to them? Why didn't you follow your heart?"

He frowns and sticks his hands in his pockets. We walk another block before he says, "I didn't want to disappoint Marianna. She had brought me to New York, shown my work when nobody knew my name. She'd given up her gallery to guide my career." He pauses, adds quietly, "Besides, she was my wife. She was pregnant with my child."

"With me," I whisper.

He nods. "I had responsibilities, Sienna. A house, a new baby. I couldn't spend the rest my life painting the colors I saw inside my head. So I went back to sculpture. My first large-scale installation was that year. It was a huge success."

The light turns red and we stop at the corner. "And that's what matters?" I ask. "Being successful?" I'm not angry now, just confused. Nothing seems certain anymore, nothing is obvious.

"It's what matters to Marianna," he says. "She can't see the point of making art for art's sake. To her, it exists to be seen, to be appreciated."

"But if the art you're creating isn't what you want, what you need—?"

"Then you take what you can get." He leans against a street lamp, hugs it with his right arm. "God," he breathes, "I'm tired."

"Let's take a cab."

He doesn't answer, but I hail one and he climbs in. He leans his head back against the seat, closes his eyes. I assume he's asleep, but the moment we pull up in front of Evelyn's Fifty-seventh Street gallery, his eyes snap open and he jumps out, alert, impatient. He's the old Hugh now, all strength and movement and purpose, and he strides into the gallery with barely a glance in my direction.

I follow him inside. The room is crowded with people, some in suits and ties or expensive dresses, others wearing leather and tattoos. There's wine and hors d'oeuvres on the table, and some kind of spacey, ambient music playing in the background. And everywhere you look, Gillian Ferris's defaced wooden sculptures—a jumble of school desks carved with initials and spray-painted gold; a bed that appears as if it was splattered with battery acid; an enormous wooden jungle gym covered with layer upon layer of chipped, faded paint.

Hugh spots Evelyn standing beside someone who must be Gillian Ferris, a tall, willowy woman with auburn-colored dreadlocks and pale skin. He heads across the room, leaving me to fend for myself. I don't mind, though, because I can't take my eyes off him. At this moment, no one would ever think he's sick. He's standing tall, smiling, charisma radiating from him like electricity. It's like when he's doing an open studio, only more intense, more mesmerizing, and I know I'm not the only one watching him. The whole room is aware of his presence.

Hugh catches Evelyn's eye, then wraps her in a bear hug as he reaches out to shake Gillian's hand. Gillian lights up like a Christmas tree when she figures out who he is, and

I can tell by the way she's looking at him that she's nervous, excited, but trying not to show it.

I move toward them, eager to hear what they're saying, but I'm distracted by two male voices behind me.

"That's Hugh Scully," the first voice says.

"I know," the second voice replies. "They're doing a retrospective of his work in L.A. next month. At the Museum of Contemporary Art."

"Did you see his last show?" the first man asks. "It was mind-blowing. Made me want to go home and torch the crap I'm working on."

The other man laughs. "Come on, let's get Gillian to introduce us. I'm going to invite him to my next studio show."

"If he likes your work, you're golden. Hugh Scully knows everybody."

The two men move past me, and soon the whole room seems to be gravitating toward Hugh, drawn by his fame, or simply his aura. He gathers them around him, charms them, holds them in his spell. Then, during a break in the conversation, he looks up and notices me standing alone. He smiles, calls my name, and motions me over.

"Sienna," he says as I approach, "I want you to meet Gillian Ferris."

Everyone turns to me. They're trying to figure out who I am, trying to decide if I'm important enough to talk to. I shake Gillian's hand and mumble something complimentary about her art. She smiles at me, then turns back to Hugh, and I'm soon forgotten again.

I listen to their conversation for a while, then wander over to the hors d'oeuvre table. As I reach for a glass of sparkling water, a handsome man in his twenties, with dark eyes and a nose ring, sidles up to me. "Hi, I'm Spencer," he says. "How do you know Hugh Scully?"

"I'm his daughter."

"No kidding. I didn't know Hugh had a daughter so

grown up, or so beautiful." He laughs, rolls his eyes. "Sorry. That came out like a bad pickup line." He leans over the table, takes an hors d'oeuvre. "Here, try the goat cheese pesto spread. It's sensational."

I smile and accept the cracker. I know he's only talking to me because of who I am, but I don't turn away, don't ignore him. The truth is, I'm enjoying the attention.

Spencer grabs a handful of chips and starts telling me about himself. He's talking a little too fast, laughing a little too loudly, and I know he's trying to charm me, hoping I'll introduce him to Hugh. "I've got a studio in Chelsea— well, it's more of a basement, really," he says with a self-deprecating chuckle. "If it isn't garbage day, I can usually catch a glimpse of sky . . ."

He goes on like that, joking, confiding in me, but after a while I realize I've stopped paying attention. I'm standing back and observing him now, judging him, a little aloof, unimpressed, amused.

And then I think about Marianna, and I wonder if it's like this for her, if she gets off on the power, the prestige of being Hugh Scully's wife. And I wonder if it's that feeling, even more than the money, that motivated her to push Hugh away from painting, to guide him toward the sculpture that's brought him success.

The thought makes me angry—at her for using Hugh's talent to make herself feel important, at me for being tempted to do the same. I turn away from Spencer, disgusted with myself, and mutter something about finding Hugh.

I spot him on the other side of the room, looking at Gillian Ferris's sculptures with Gillian, Evelyn, and a group of admirers, all eager to hear his opinion and parrot it back at him. He's holding a glass of wine in his right hand and his eyes are shining, his features animated. At that moment, someone hands him a plate of hors d'oeuvres. He reaches out with his left hand, but his fingers don't close tightly enough around the plate and it falls, shattering against Gillian's school desk sculpture.

Hugh curses, turns quickly to the left, and bumps into a woman standing beside him. "Sorry," he mutters. He strides over to the hors d'oeuvre table, leaving Evelyn and her assistants to clean up the mess, and pours himself more wine.

"Go easy there, Hugh," a man says with a chuckle, but I know my father hasn't been drinking much, and he definitely isn't drunk. It's the tumor that's making him weak, that's throwing him off balance.

Hugh responds to the man's remark by filling his glass to the brim and drinking deeply. He walks away, bumping against the corner of the table as he goes.

"Are you all right?" I whisper, hurrying over to join him.

"I'm fine. Terrific." He gulps down some more wine and heads back toward Evelyn and Gillian. He's swaying a little, putting one foot slowly in front of the other. I follow a few steps behind, not quite knowing what to think, what to do.

Evelyn intercepts him before he gets to Gillian, and puts her arm around his waist. "What's the matter, Hugh?" she asks with a worried smile. "Did you have a few too many?"

"Something like that." He downs the rest of his wine, rubs his left eye. "Evelyn, I want you to promise me something."

"What is it?"

"Any art I make during the next few months, don't sell it. You understand? No matter what I create, it's not for sale."

"But why?"

"Just do as I say," he tells her. "That includes the installation I'm working on now. I don't want you to sell it, or even show it."

"But Hugh, the piece you're working on now is going in the retrospective. After that, I thought—"

"Don't think," he snaps, grabbing her upper arms and pulling her toward him. "Just promise me you'll do what I ask. Please, Evelyn. *Please*."

She stares at him with wide, frightened eyes. "All right, Hugh," she breathes. "I promise."

Hugh lets out a long breath, then leaves us and walks unsteadily toward Gillian Ferris. He says a few words to her, leans over to kiss her cheek, but instead loses his balance and falls forward.

The crowd lets out a tiny gasp, but Hugh recovers just in time to clasp Gillian in a clumsy embrace. She laughs uncomfortably and waits to be released, but he continues hugging her, not moving, not speaking, for what seems like forever. Everyone is watching, exchanging glances, and I've never been so embarrassed, so sorry for someone, and so scared, all at the same time.

Then at last Hugh steps back, turns, and walks through the crowd to join me. "Do you want to sit down?" I ask anxiously.

"What I want is to get the hell out of here," he growls.

He takes my arm and the crowd separates to let us pass. Then he pushes open the door and the cold wind hits my face, making my nose run and giving me an excuse for the tears that fill my eyes.

Chapter 17

It's dark now and Hugh's staggering down Fifty-seventh Street, squinting as the wind hits his face. I can't tell if it's the tumor that's making him move like this, or if the wine he drank is starting to affect him. All I know is that he's unsteady, out of control, and it's scaring me.

"Let's get a cab," I say, hurrying after him. "Do you have a key to Evelyn's house?"

He shakes his head, keeps walking. "I don't want to go back there." His voice is gravelly, his words slightly slurred.

"Then let's find the car. Let's get out of here."

He doesn't respond, doesn't even look at me. Just keeps moving, seeming not to notice the other people on the sidewalk who are hugging the curb to stay out of his way.

"It's so damned easy," he mutters as we reach the corner.

"What is?" I ask.

"Impressing people, making them think you've got something to say."

"But why shouldn't people be impressed by you?" I ask. "You're an amazing artist. They respect you."

"It's not about respect," he says. "It's about power. Who's on top this year." He shakes his head. "I can play that game. I'm a master. But I don't enjoy it anymore."

"Then why do you do it?" I ask.

"Habit, I guess." He looks over at me. "It feels good to be admired, Sienna, to be well-paid and in demand. Much better than being poor and unknown."

"That's not what you used to think back when you were teaching up in Boston. Anyway, if you have to give up what you love to find success—"

"Then you're a sell-out," he says flatly. "A bullshit artist." He laughs bitterly at his unintentional pun. "And you know what?" he tells me. "For a long time, I didn't even care."

I don't want to hear him talk that way, don't want to think of him as a willing participant in Marianna's schemes of fame and fortune. "You couldn't help it," I remind him. "You had responsibilities. A wife, a new house. You had me."

"I wasn't thinking about any of that—not after I got my first real taste of success. I was thinking about myself, my own desires. I was feeding my ego."

His words sting like salt water on a wound. "And now?" I ask, desperately trying not to let him see how much his answer matters to me. "What about now?"

"Now it's too late. I pissed away my time, Sienna, and I'm out of luck."

He looks over at me and our eyes meet, like two frightened animals stumbling upon each other in the forest. Then suddenly, he turns his back on me, cuts across the middle of the street, and takes off down Fifth Avenue. He's heading away from Evelyn's house, away from the car, and suddenly I realize where he's going.

"The museum's closed," I call, jogging after him.

"No it's not," he snaps. "It can't be." He starts to run, but he's listing to the left, toward the storefronts.

"I saw the sign. It closed at six."

"Shut up," he orders, running faster, swaying like a boxer who's taken a hit. "Just shut up."

He careens into a store window, stumbles to his knees, then scrambles up and keeps running. I catch up to him and grab his arm, but he shakes me off as easily as a horse shaking off a fly, and I'm startled to realize how strong he is even in this condition, and how helpless I feel.

Then we reach Fifty-third Street and he turns the corner. The museum is up ahead, its colorful banners snapping in the wind. He runs up to the doors and tries to pull them open. But they're locked, of course, and there's no one inside.

"Let me in!" he shouts, banging his fists against the glass. "I want to see the Kandinskys!"

Just minutes ago, Hugh was surrounded by a crowd of admirers. Now passersby are glancing at him with alarm; people are ducking their heads and crossing the street to avoid him. "Hugh," I plead, trying not to let him see my embarrassment, "let's go. We can come back tomorrow."

"I don't give a shit about tomorrow. I want to see them now. Right *now*."

A white-haired security guard appears in the lobby. Hugh spots him and starts banging again. "Open the doors!" he demands. "Let me in!"

The guard frowns, then takes the walkie-talkie from his belt and speaks into it. When he's finished, he walks up to Hugh and calls through the glass, "Sir, I'm going to have to ask you to leave."

Hugh laughs as if that's the funniest thing he's ever heard. "Don't you know who I am?" he asks. "I'm Hugh Scully. The museum owns two of my sculptures, for God's sake."

"Yes, sir. I've called the police and if you're not gone in two minutes, I'm afraid they're going to—"

"Let me in!" Hugh bellows. He hauls back and throws a punch at the guard, but his fist hits the glass door with a thud. The impact startles him and his face goes blank. Then the pain comes. His holds his hand, lets out a groan, and slides slowly to the sidewalk.

"Hugh," I plead, kneeling down beside him, "let's get out of here." That's when I notice the glistening tracks on his cheeks. My stomach clenches as I realize they're tears. He's crying, but no sound is coming out.

"The vision in my left eye has been getting worse for weeks," he says in a husky voice. "Tonight, at the gallery, I couldn't see a damned thing from here over." He sweeps his hand from his left eye to his ear, and laughs in disbelief. "I'm going blind, Sienna."

I stare at him, too shocked to speak, to think. Then the guard taps on the glass with his knuckles, motions for me to move Hugh away from the doors. But how? I can't carry him, probably couldn't even drag him if he didn't want to go.

Just then, I spot a taxi cruising down the block. Incredibly, it's empty. I jump up and dash into the street, waving my arms wildly. The driver hits the brakes and sticks his head out of the window. "You got a death wish or something, kid?"

"I need a cab. Please. It's an emergency."

He looks me over, unimpressed. "Get in."

I run back to Hugh. "Come on, we're leaving." I grab his wrists and pull as hard as I can. He staggers to his feet and allows me to lead him to the cab. I open the back door and we both try to get in at the same time, bumping heads in the process.

The bump—the most trivial screw-up of the entire screwed-up evening—is so absurd that he starts to laugh, softly at first, then louder. I'm laughing too, half-hysterical, barely able to catch my breath.

"After you," he says, bowing so low I'm afraid he's going to fall over.

"No, you go ahead."

"No, you."

"Hugh, *get in*," I insist, pushing him toward the door.

He collapses into the cab and half slides, half crawls across the seat, still laughing like a maniac. I get in after him.

"Where to?" the driver asks, eyeing us disdainfully in the rearview mirror.

"Eighty-ninth and Park," I say, stifling an out-of-control giggle.

He takes off, and I stare out the window, sucking in deep breaths, trying hard to calm myself. When I finally turn to Hugh, he's crumpled in the corner, head bouncing against the window, asleep.

Chapter 18

When we get near Eighty-ninth Street, I tell the cab driver to circle the block. I spot the Range Rover and we pull over. Hugh is still asleep and I have to shake him hard to wake him up. He looks groggy, disoriented, and it takes him two tries to count out the money for the driver.

We get out of the cab and I ask Hugh for the car keys. There's no way he can drive; the way he's acting, I wouldn't even trust him to read a map. While he rummages in his pockets, I watch the cars roaring up and down Park Avenue, swerving from lane to lane, honking their horns. I've done a fair amount of driving back home with Marianna in the car, but I've never driven in Manhattan before, never driven in any city bigger than Trenton, New Jersey.

"Hugh," I say anxiously, "I don't know if I can—"

My voice trails off. He's not listening. He's leaning against the back fender, head bowed and eyes closed.

"Are you all right?" I ask.

He opens his eyes. "My head is throbbing."

"Maybe you should see a doctor."

"Why? So he can tell me I have a brain tumor?"

"Then let's go back to Evelyn's house. You need to lie down."

"I'm going to the island, Sienna," he says, walking toward me.

"We can go tomorrow. Right now you should—"

He lunges forward and grabs my wrist. "Are you going to drive me, or shall I drive myself?"

I look into his eyes. They're dark, determined. He'll do it, I know he will. But how far will he get before he loses control, maybe crashes the car?

"I'll drive," I say.

He releases my wrist and I unlock the car. Hugh opens the back door and stretches out across the seat. That's when I realize my duffel bag is still in Evelyn's house. "The bags," I tell him. "We left them at Evelyn's."

"So what?" he mutters.

"But my clothes, my toothbrush—"

He doesn't answer and when I look in the back seat I see that he's staring out the window, oblivious. So I get in the car, reminding myself that what we don't have on the island we can buy in Teal Harbor, and that my most important possession—my sketchbook—is in the backpack lying beside me on the front seat.

I put the key in the ignition and start the engine, unable to forget that the last time I drove I had a driver's ed. instructor sitting next to me with his own set of controls. I take a deep breath and ease out onto Park Avenue, driving slowly, attentively, my eyes darting between the double yellow line, the parked cars, and the traffic lights down the block.

The one thing I've forgotten is the other drivers, and when a delivery truck cuts in front of me, my heart leaps into my throat and I slam on the brakes. The guy behind me honks and swerves around me, and I half expect a cop to appear and slap me with a ticket. It doesn't happen, though, so I continue until the next red light, wondering why Hugh is being so quiet.

When I turn around, my heart skips a beat because he's lying half on the seat, half on the floor, eyes closed, twisted and corpselike. Then I see his chest gently rising and falling and I realize he's asleep.

The light turns green and I keep driving, first a little too fast, then a little too slow, my foot constantly jumping between the accelerator and the brake. The cross streets drift by—101st, 102nd, 103rd—and I notice the buildings are getting shabbier, the vacant lots more frequent. The people on the sidewalk are eyeing me suspiciously, and I find myself counting the seconds until each red light turns green.

Then I see a sign for the New York Thruway, and I figure that will get me out of the city, so I cross a bridge and head onto the highway. I'm hugging the right lane, driving about forty miles an hour, and everybody's passing me, but I don't care. I'm just moving forward, trying to stay between the dotted white lines, trying not to crash.

After what seems like forever, a motel's neon sign comes into view, a shimmering oasis in an asphalt desert. It's almost nine o'clock and I feel wasted. I can't think of anything I'd rather do than sink down between some crisp, white sheets and close my eyes.

I glance over my shoulder at Hugh. He's totally out of it and probably won't wake up for hours. I picture myself slipping his wallet out of his pants, renting a room, and catching a few hours of sleep. By the time he wakes up, I tell myself, we'll be on the road again.

But no sooner does the idea cross my mind than I reject it—not only because I don't want to leave Hugh alone, but because I don't know what might happen if he wakes up and finds himself in a motel parking lot. I imagine him stumbling into the lobby, dizzy and confused, shouting my name like a drunk on a bender. Or worse yet, creating a humiliating scene in the parking lot—maybe breaking down the motel room door, then grabbing the keys and driving off, clipping a couple of parked cars in the process.

The realization that Hugh might do something to embarrass me—that he already *has* embarrassed me—hits me hard because I used to be so eager to be seen with him, so proud to tell people I was his daughter. But that was back when he still seemed strong, in charge, practically invincible.

Tears fill my eyes, blurring the white line in the road. I think about the hours of driving still ahead of us, about Birch Cove Island, miles away from the nearest doctor or hospital. I picture our ramshackle cabin with no heat or electricity, the wood-burning barrel stove and the stone well where we haul up water with a bucket, and I try to imagine how Hugh will handle it all. What if he can't walk, can't see, can't think clearly? Will I be able to take care of him?

But what really scares me is that it's not just Hugh's body that seems to be collapsing before my eyes. It's his soul, his very being. And I wonder, is the tumor affecting his personality, or is it just my perception of him that's changing? I'm not sure. All I know is that my powerful, confident father doesn't seem so powerful anymore, and I dread the prospect of hearing any more stories from the past, uncovering any new truths, being privy to any further revelations.

A green sign looms over my head, pointing the way to Connecticut, and all I once I know I can't handle this. I can't drive Hugh to Maine, can't take care of him, can't watch him fall apart. I need someone strong to step in and take over, someone who knows how to handle Hugh, who knows how to take charge.

I need Marianna.

An exit appears and I take it. It leads me onto a two-lane road, lined with shopping centers and industrial parks. I pull into the empty parking lot of a minimall. The stores—a deli, a hair salon, and a pet shop—are closed, but there's a pay phone in front of the deli. Hugh's still asleep, so I get out and walk to the phone, trying to imagine what Marianna is doing right now, what she's thinking.

I picture her in the farmhouse, maybe sitting in her office, or talking on the phone. I know she must have caught the first plane out of Houston when Liesel told her we were missing. She must be worried sick about us. But when I picture her face, all I can see is disappointment. And when I imagine her voice, it sounds impatient and exasperated.

"What possessed you to take off with him, Sienna?" I hear her saying. "You should have called me immediately. All right, listen carefully. I want you to drive him to the nearest hospital, then have the doctor call me collect. Is there a phone book there, Sienna? Look in the Yellow Pages under hospitals and read me the options."

My fantasy seems so real, so very likely, that I turn around and walk back to the car, unable to face her disdain. Then I see my backpack lying on the seat, and suddenly it hits me that I haven't sketched anything for almost twenty-four hours. Like a diver surfacing for air, I pull out my sketchbook and pencils. They feel so comfortable in my hands, so right, and I look around eagerly for something to draw.

But tonight my usual subjects—a crumpled candy wrapper in a muddy puddle, my knee resting against the fender of the Range Rover, the finches in the pet shop window—don't satisfy me. I begin each sketch, stop, then start another, until all at once I find myself drawing the wine bottle on Evelyn Fadulo's dining room table.

I never draw from memory, but tonight my sketch of Evelyn's table seems effortless, like a photograph developing before my eyes. I sketch Evelyn's guest bed with the white linens, and Hugh's painting hanging over it. Then my half-eaten pastrami sandwich sitting on the worn deli table; Gillian Ferris's defaced school desks; the entrance to the Museum of Modern Art.

I look up, exhausted and exhilarated, and my eyes are drawn to Hugh's limp body draped across the back seat. I never draw portraits, but with his collar turned up, his face hidden, and his left arm twisted beneath him, he's more a still life than a human being, and I'm filled with a desire to try.

I put my pencil to the paper, but at that moment he lets out a stuttering sigh and rolls onto his back. I can see his face now, the delicate blue veins on his eyelids, the gray stubble on his chin, the soft flesh hanging loose beneath his jaw. He looks older than his sixty years, weak and vulnerable, a human being again. My father.

And all at once I know I'm not going to call Marianna. I'm going to finish what I started, what I agreed to do. I'm going to take Hugh to Birch Cove Island.

At that moment, Hugh's body tenses and he begins to twitch. I know immediately what's happening. It's a seizure, just like the one he had outside the studio almost two months ago. But this time Marianna isn't here to take charge, to give orders, to send me away. This time whatever happens is up to me.

I throw open the car door, kneel down on the floor, and wrap my arms around him. "You're going to be all right," I whisper, holding him tight, pressing my head against his trembling chest. "It's almost over. Just hang on."

I stay like that until the shaking stops, until his body goes limp and his breathing becomes deep and regular. Then I put away my sketchbook, get into the driver's seat, and start the car.

Chapter 19

I drive to the nearest gas station and pull in. I'm asking the cashier for directions to the hospital when I see Hugh sit up in the back seat. He's holding his head and squinting uncertainly into the lights. I wait impatiently for the guy to finish his directions, then jog back to the car.

"How do you feel?" I ask.

He doesn't answer, just looks blankly out of the window. "Where are we?"

"Somewhere between Manhattan and the Connecticut border. You had another seizure. I'm taking you to the hospital."

To my surprise, he doesn't argue, just groans and sinks back into the seat.

I drive through the darkness, my hands gripping the steering wheel so tightly that when I finally see the lights of the hospital and pull into the emergency room parking lot, I can barely straighten out my fingers. I turn around to look at Hugh, but he's already opening the car door, stumbling as he gets out.

We make our way to the emergency room, Hugh limping, me walking anxiously beside him, like a coach spotting a gymnast on a balance beam. The waiting room is practically empty—no patients in sight—and so white, so blazingly bright that I feel like I'm in some Hollywood filmmaker's version of the future.

Then the receptionist turns to us, and suddenly Hugh is standing a little straighter, smiling, holding his head up high. I stare at him, blown away by his ability to pull himself together, to maintain his dignity even while his body is failing him. But when he speaks, his performance starts to unravel.

"My head hurts," he mutters thickly. "It's . . . something happened. I can't remember." He turns to me. "Sienna?"

"My father was diagnosed with a brain tumor about two months ago," I explain. "He had a seizure tonight, about twenty minutes ago."

"That's right," Hugh agrees. "And now I have an agonizing headache. I need . . . something. I need . . . " His voice trails off and he looks to me again for help.

"Something for the pain."

Hugh nods and the receptionist looks him over, maybe wondering if he's actually a drug addict hoping to score some downers. "I have a few forms for you to fill out," she says at last. "And can I make a copy of your insurance card?"

Hugh takes the forms and we sit down on white plastic chairs. He tries to grip the pen, grimaces, and asks, "Why does my hand hurt?"

"You punched the glass in front of the Museum of Modern Art."

"Ah, yes." He lets out a weary sigh, tries again, but his handwriting is shaky and he's having trouble steadying the clipboard with his left hand.

"I'll do it," I say.

As I reach for the pen, I notice a small, dark stain in the crotch of his pants. The fabric looks damp and at first I'm baffled. Then I realize he must have wet himself during the seizure, and I feel so sorry for him, so embarrassed. I want to slip my arms around him and hug him tight, but there's still a wall between us, an invisible barrier that keeps me rooted to my seat.

Then a nurse appears. "Mr. Scully?" she asks.

Hugh gets slowly to his feet, wincing with pain. I start to stand up too, but he shakes his head, motions me back into my seat. "Wait here," he says, and even now, when Hugh seems so helpless, so vulnerable, I don't think to question him.

He follows the nurse through a set of double doors and I sit there for what seems like hours, reading a month-old copy of *Newsweek* over and over again, never actually comprehending a word of it. Eventually I decide to get my sketchbook, to draw something. But as soon as I stand up, a man appears, tall and plump, with smooth, pink cheeks and a small, crooked smile.

"You're Mr. Scully's daughter?" he asks.

"Yes."

"I'm Dr. Lipmann. Your father tells me you're traveling home to Pennsylvania tonight."

Is that what Hugh said? Does he really want to go home, I wonder, or is he lying, telling the doctor what he wants to hear? I nod noncommittally. "How is he?"

"We administered an anti-seizure medication intravenously. He's feeling a bit groggy and lethargic, which is to be expected. I suggest you get him home as soon as possible, then have your mother call his neurologist the first thing tomorrow morning."

I want to ask more, so much more. Is Hugh really going blind? Will he lose the use of his left arm, his leg, his mind? Is he really going to die? But I'm still struggling to formulate the first question, still trying to get up the courage to put my dread into words, when the double doors swing open and Hugh appears, sitting in a wheelchair being pushed by the nurse.

I meet my father's eye and force myself to smile, but he doesn't respond. He's slumped against the left armrest, his shoulders stooped, his eyes glazed over. The nurse wheels him toward me and I reach for the handles, but she shakes her head. "I have to take him as far as the door," she says. "Hospital policy."

"He'll probably sleep most of the way home," Dr. Lipmann tells me. "You'd better drive your car up to the door so you can help him in. And don't forget, he needs to see his doctor tomorrow. He should be taking his medications regularly. That's the only way to prevent further seizures." He smiles his crooked smile. "Any questions?"

The moment has passed. I shake my head and he looks relieved. I hurry out to the car and drive it around to the door. The nurse is waiting, and together we guide Hugh into the back seat.

As I drive away, I glance at him in the rearview mirror. "How do you feel?"

His voice is hoarse, and the words come out slowly. "Like I'm drifting. Floating above the car." He pauses. "Sienna?" he calls, as if he's searching for me in a fog bank.

"I'm here," I say.

"Take me to the island."

"You're sure?"

"Yes." He pauses. "Can you follow the birds?"

"What?"

"If we're going to fly there," he says, "we have to follow the birds."

A shiver runs through me as I realize he's spaced out, stoned from the medicine the doctor gave him. "Okay," I say, and I know my voice sounds forced and cheery, like I'm talking to a small child. "We'll follow the birds."

But Hugh doesn't answer and when I glance at him again he's curled up on the seat, eyes closed, a blissed-out smile on his face, and I know he's soaring above the clouds on his way to Birch Cove Island.

Chapter 20

I drive for most of the night, not really knowing the way but afraid that if I stop for directions I'll lose my nerve and turn around. Instead, I just follow the signs, taking any exit that says Massachusetts, then New Hampshire, then Maine.

Hugh sleeps most of the way, but even when he's awake he's not really present, not truly himself. He lies on his back, gazing out the window at the stars, muttering about clouds and birds and wind currents. Once he sits up and sticks his arms out like he's flying. "Don't crash," he warns. "Watch it now, watch it!"

"Okay," I reply, trying not to let him hear the alarm in my voice, trying to sound reassuring. "I'll be careful."

In response, he laughs heartily and flings his head back against the head rest. A moment later, he's curled up on the seat again, asleep.

After Portland, things start to look familiar. I take Route

1 and head up the coast. The sky is clouding over, obscuring the stars, and a wild wind sends dead leaves skittering across the windshield. A few miles later, it starts to drizzle. I turn on the wipers and drive slower, even more cautiously, my heart pounding in time to the wiper blades' rhythmic chant.

The black sky is fading to a pale grayish-orange by the time we finally arrive in Teal Harbor. The parking lot at the wharf is empty, except for a few pickup trucks with boat trailers attached. I park in the far corner, away from the docks and the bait store and Maggie's Morning Call Café.

When I turn off the engine, the power seems to drain out of my body as well. I rest my head against the window and close my eyes, and within seconds I'm asleep. It's a deep sleep, dark and dreamless, and I don't remember anything until I feel a hand shaking my shoulder and a soft, insistent voice saying, "Sienna, wake up."

I open my eyes to find Hugh sitting beside me in the front seat. His hair is mussed, his clothes are wrinkled, and he smells of sweat and dried urine, but his eyes are alert and I know he's in there now. He's Hugh Scully again.

"What time is it?" I ask, looking around. It's raining for real now and the windsock hanging from the bait shop porch is twisting and flapping like a netted fish.

"Almost eight o'clock," he replies.

"How long have you been awake?"

"I don't know. Two, maybe three hours."

His voice is unusually flat and subdued and his body seems oddly still. His eyes are focused and intent, but in a different way than they used to be. They reflect a quiet energy, directed inward instead of out toward the world.

"How do you feel?" I ask.

"The drugs are wearing off and my headache's back. But at least I can think clearly again." He gazes out the window at the rain. "That's what I've been doing while you were asleep. Thinking."

"About what?"

"Come on," he says, ignoring my question, "let's get some breakfast and see if we can find a fisherman who's heading out toward the island."

I open the door and the cold rain hits my face. Hugh is halfway across the parking lot. He's still limping, but today he's walking in a straight line, not stumbling or weaving. I grab my backpack and follow him, head bowed, water dripping down my neck.

Hugh opens the door of Maggie's Morning Call and a blast of warm air envelops me; the smell of bacon and toast fills my nostrils. In summertime, Maggie's is crowded with tourists, but this morning there are only a few customers—five or six fishermen at the counter, a few businessmen at the tables. As we walk in, they all turn to look at us. We're not locals and they know it.

Hugh selects a table by the window and we sit down. He orders coffee and rye toast. I order eggs, bacon, potatoes, and a big glass of milk. When the coffee comes, Hugh lifts the cup awkwardly to his lips. A few drops splash onto his left sleeve, but he doesn't seem to notice.

"Did they give you a prescription for the anti-seizure medicine at the hospital?" I ask.

"Um-hum," he replies, gazing out the window. "Painkillers, too. I'm not going to fill them though."

"Why not?"

"You saw what the medicine did to me. I was in outer space. From now on, I want to be completely clear, completely focused."

"But what about the headaches? What if you have another seizure?"

"The headaches are what's going to keep me from losing my nerve. As for the seizures, I'll take the risk."

I don't understand what he's talking about but I'm distracted by the arrival of the food. I can barely get the eggs into my mouth fast enough, but Hugh isn't eating. He's watching the fishermen at the counter. They're all middle-aged or older, with weathered faces and thinning hair, except for a young man at the end, a tall, broad-shouldered guy not much older than me, with a wide face and brown hair that curls around his ears and over his collar.

Hugh takes another sip of coffee, then stands up and walks toward them. They fall silent as he approaches.

"Any of you sailing out toward Birch Cove Island today?" he asks.

"Not sailing anywhere today," replies a gaunt, white-haired man with pale blue eyes.

"I'll make it worth your while," Hugh continues, undaunted. "How about fifty dollars?"

"Seen the sky?" asks a husky man in a blue wool cap.

"Of course, but—"

"This storm's just getting warmed up," the white-haired man says.

The young man at the end of the counter nods. "The waves are big and getting bigger. Rain'll probably turn to sleet by nightfall."

"I've got to get to Birch Cove today," Hugh insists. "I'll pay anyone who takes me there a hundred dollars."

"You're the fella who lives out there in summer, aintcha?" says Maggie, wiping her wrinkled hands on her apron as she steps out of the kitchen. "The artist, right?"

"Uh-huh."

"Whatdaya want going out there this time of year?" she asks. "Ain't vacation weather, ya know."

"I realize that," Hugh says impatiently. He turns back to the fishermen. "Two hundred dollars. That's my final offer."

"Come back the day after tomorrow," the man in the wool hat remarks with a wry smile. "I'll gladly take you for two hundred dollars then." The others chuckle and nod in agreement.

"There's a nice B&B up in Rockland," a red-headed fisherman mutters around his pipe. "Why not relax a couple of days, maybe take in the sights?"

Maggie and the other fishermen laugh, but Hugh isn't amused. "I'm going to Birch Cove, and I'm going today," he growls. "If none of you have the balls to take me, then I'll damn well find someone who will."

He walks back to our table and tosses his wallet down. "Pay the bill, Sienna," he orders. "I'll be outside."

He heads for the door and I count out the money. As I stand up, the young fisherman catches my eye. He's not laughing now, and the expression on his face is thoughtful, concerned—or at least, that's how it strikes me. Before I can decide for sure, he turns back to his coffee and I head outside.

Chapter 21

I find Hugh pacing up and down the wharf, eyes flitting left and right, like an animal in a cage. There's no one else in sight, no boats on the water, and the sea looks gray and angry.

"Let's go find that bed and breakfast," I suggest, falling into step beside him. "We can come back tomorrow."

"Tomorrow you're supposed to be in school."

It takes me a second to comprehend what he's talking about. Right now school seems as remote and foreign as the face of the moon. "And you're supposed to be in your studio, working on your new installation," I say. "What's that got to do with anything?"

He shakes his head vigorously. "I can't go back there, and I sure as hell can't go on like this." He stares down at the wooden slats of the wharf. Beneath our feet, the gray-green water churns and swirls.

Suddenly, Hugh takes off, jogging across the wharf and

down to the docks. Four skiffs with oars under the seats and outboard motors at the stern are tied to metal belaying cleats. He jumps awkwardly into one of them, almost tipping it over.

"Hey, what are you doing?" I cry, hurrying after him.

"What's it look like?" He pulls the choke and turns the throttle to start, then grabs the starter line and yanks on it. It's something that would have been simple for him to do a few months ago, but today he can barely pull the rope twelve inches. The engine sputters weakly, then falls silent.

"Hugh, please," I beg. "If those fishermen won't take us, we'd be crazy to risk it in a skiff. Besides, you don't even know who that belongs to."

"It belongs to me," a voice says behind us. I spin around to see the young fisherman striding toward us. He's wearing yellow rain gear and worn leather boots with rubber soles. "You planning on stealing my boat?" he asks Hugh.

"He's getting out," I say. "You don't have to call the cops or anything, okay?"

The fisherman laughs. "I wasn't planning on it. That is, unless stealing my skiff is more appealing to you than hitching a ride in my lobster boat."

"You'll take me out to the island?" Hugh asks, looking up.

"Well, I can see you're going to try to get out there one way or another. I'd rather take you myself than have to fish you out of the ocean later." He hops nimbly into the boat. "Name's Caleb Hanlon," he says, holding out his hand.

"Hugh Scully."

Caleb nods. They shake hands and he turns to me expectantly.

"I'm Sienna," I say.

He smiles. "My boat's moored just outside the harbor. If you don't mind a few waves breaking in your lap, I'll have you there in less than five minutes." He reaches out a hand, palm up, to help me into the skiff.

"No," Hugh says. "She's not coming."

"What?" I gasp.

Hugh grabs the edge of the dock and drags himself out of the skiff. "Hang on a minute," he tells Caleb. He leads me away from the skiff and says, "I've taken you away from your own life for too long. It's time you went home."

"But I don't want to go home," I insist. "I want to be with you."

"No, Sienna. What I'm going to do out there, I've got to do alone."

"What are you talking about?" I look into his eyes. They've got that same quiet energy I saw earlier, the same inward focus. Then he smiles, and his face is almost radiant.

"When we left the farmhouse," he says, "I wasn't sure why I was going to Birch Cove Island. I just knew I wanted to be there, that it felt right. But now I understand. It's where I'm going to die."

"But that could be months from now," I argue, "maybe years if you go to Houston and take those drug treatments."

"It won't be months, or even weeks," he says quietly. "I'm going to die when I choose to die, Sienna, and I'll do it by my own hand."

"Suicide?" I cry in disbelief, and my voice sounds pinched and ridiculous, like a cartoon character.

Hugh doesn't answer, just gazes past me like I wasn't there. I want to shake him, shove him into the icy water, anything to make him look at me, to keep him present. But I don't have that kind of influence over him.

"Marianna won't let you," I tell him. "She says you have to keep working. You can't give in to your illness."

Invoking my mother's name has the desired effect. Hugh's looking at me now, his eyes flashing. "Marianna figured out how to control my art, but the rest of my life belongs to me."

"But you have to listen to her. She knows what you need. She knows—"

"She knows *nothing*," he snaps. "If I want to get bombed, or sleep with beautiful women, or blow my brains out, I'm going to do it. She's never been able to stop me and she can't stop me now."

I stare at him, stunned into silence. What's he telling me? That kissing Evelyn Fadulo wasn't a stress-induced aberration? That he's been sleeping with her and who knows how many other women for years? I take the information and try to cram it into one of those little boxes inside my head, but it won't fit. I can't close the lid and stack it on the shelf, can't make Hugh's words disappear.

"Sienna," he says, ignoring the wiped-clean look on my face, "thank you for bringing me here. I'm glad we had this time together, but now you have to go. What happens from here on in, you don't want to see."

He takes an awkward step toward me and holds out his arms. *He's going to hug me*, I suddenly realize, and I stiffen, amazed and appalled, as he slips his arms around me. He feels my tenseness and responds instantly, barely touching me before he pulls away. Then he turns, walks back across the dock, and climbs into the skiff.

I stand there, paralyzed, too demolished to move. It takes the roar of the outboard motor to bring me back, to remind my brain to tell my body to function. And now I'm running across the dock, shouting, "Hugh, wait! Don't go!"

Caleb has already untied the skiff and he's pulling away from the dock, pointing the bow into the oncoming chop. He turns when he hears my voice, his forehead furrowed, his eyes questioning.

I feel like shrieking and pulling out my hair. I want to leap off the dock and drag the skiff back with my bare hands. But instead I merely lift one hand and whimper, "No. Please, no."

Then my father leans over and says something into Caleb's ear, and now Caleb is smiling and waving, convinced that I'm waving too, that I'm wishing them a speedy journey, a fond farewell. He turns back toward the bow, cranks the throttle, and takes off, leaving a spray of whitewater behind him. I stand there, my arm still stuck in the air like some damaged scarecrow, watching them fly through the water, until they disappear into the rain and the wind and the waves, until they're gone.

PART III

The Island

PART II

Chapter 22

I'm supposed to be sad, I tell myself, staring out at the line where heaving gray ocean dissolves into dripping gray sky. *I'm supposed to feel sorrow.*

But what I feel is furious. I've been betrayed, used, then dumped when I was no longer needed. And what burns me the most is that it's been so easy for Hugh to accomplish. No sweet talk required, no promises of fatherly love, no need to lay on the guilt. All he had to say was, "I want to go up to the island. I want you to come with me," and I was ready and willing—desperately eager, in fact—to sign on as his chauffeur, his nurse, his confidante and accomplice.

And now he wants to leave me behind. But I refuse to be discarded so easily. I won't go home like some obedient puppy with her tail tucked between her legs. I'm going to follow Hugh. I'm going to get to that island if I have to swim there.

But of course I don't have to swim because there are still three skiffs tied to the dock. I jump into the nearest one and study the outboard motor. It's not much different from our own skiff, the one we use to go fishing in the summer. Unlike Hugh, I have no problem yanking the starter rope, and the engine quickly purrs to life.

I untie the skiff and chug away from the dock, trying to remember exactly which way Caleb went. There are no landmarks to help me; it's too rainy and gray to make out the lobster boats moored outside the harbor, too choppy to pay attention to anything except the swells rising before me like hills on a roller coaster. Still, the thought of turning back doesn't occur to me. I'm too caught up in my own thoughts to be scared, too focused on the horizon to have second thoughts.

Leaning forward, squinting into the wind and the rain, a mental slide show of the last two days begins flashing inside my head. I see Hugh kissing Evelyn; I hear him spit out the words, "This doesn't concern you." I see him careening up Fifty-seventh Street, spouting his pathetic excuses for why he can't paint anymore, why he gets off on having people admire him, why he traded in his muse for money. Then I see him standing on the dock just minutes ago, assuring me, "I'm glad we spent this time together," as if we were strangers who happened to be seated next to each other on a bus, not father and daughter about to be separated forever.

I came on this trip with modest expectations. All I wanted was an opportunity to connect with my father, a chance to glimpse who he really is, deep down inside.

"Well, I got what I wanted," I mutter into the white noise of the engine and the wind. "I've seen who Hugh really is. A sell-out. An adulterer. An insincere shit."

Tears fill my eyes as I think back to the way it used to be, when Hugh seemed like a god to me, a superman.

When I used to hide in the shadows, gazing at him with timid adoration.

But did that man, the Hugh Scully I worshipped, ever exist? No, I decide. He was just a fantasy I created, an imaginary deity I put up on a pedestal to be admired and feared, but never truly known.

Hugh isn't a god, I tell myself, never was. He's a man, that's all, a weak, flawed human being. And suddenly there are fresh images running in my head, and I see him dropping the plate of hors d'oeuvres at Evelyn's gallery, crying in front of the Museum of Modern Art, lying in the back of the Range Rover, his body racked with spasms.

The images fade and I feel a sudden rush of sympathy, of forgiveness. No matter how hard Hugh tries, he can't fight the tumor that's burrowing into his brain. He can't fight death. But that doesn't explain why he can't resist the lure of fame and money, does it? Or the taste of Evelyn Fadulo's lips.

I try to picture my father touching other women, undressing them, lying beside them. It makes my stomach turn. *How could he do that to my mother*, I wonder indignantly, *to his wife?*

Just then, I spot something white bobbing in the distance. It's a boat and I head for it, shouting, "Hugh! Caleb!" But as I draw near, I see it isn't a lobster boat. It's a long green shrimp boat with heavy nets drooping from the mast.

My heart sinks and I begin to wonder what I'm doing out here, what I'm trying to prove. Then I remember what Hugh said to me before he sailed away in Caleb's skiff. *If I want to get bombed, or sleep with beautiful women, or blow my brains out, I'm going to do it.*

"Not this time, Hugh," I whisper. "This time I'm calling your bluff."

I open the throttle and roar away from the fishing boat, scanning the horizon for something familiar. But there are no other vessels in sight, no buoys or markers. Just then, a wave breaks over the bow of the skiff, drenching my jeans. The cold water brings me back to the present, to reality, and I realize the wind has grown stronger and the swells are turning into choppy breakers. I'm completely lost, with no idea how to find Caleb's lobster boat, or the island, or even the wharf.

Panic clutches me and I spin the skiff around, trying to remember which direction I came from. A gust of wind pushes me parallel to the swells and a wave hits me broadside, tipping the skiff so violently that I have to clutch the gunwale to keep from tumbling out.

The skiff slides down the back of the wave and I grab the throttle and gun the engine, turning the bow so the swells are rolling in behind me, praying I'm headed back toward the docks. I'm not thinking about Hugh now. I'm not thinking about anything except survival. I plow through the water, zigzagging left, then right, straining my eyes as I stare into the rain and the spray, searching for something, anything that isn't sky or water.

And then I see it—a line of dim lights shining in the distance. Laughing with relief, I steer the waterlogged skiff toward them and gradually the wharf comes into view. I ease around it, toward the docks, and shift the engine into neutral. Now I can hear the sound of gruff voices, and I see two figures dressed in yellow raingear climbing into skiffs. It's two of the fishermen from Maggie's Morning Call, and an instant later, they spot me too.

"What in God's name—?" cries the man with the gaunt face, his pale blue eyes scowling into the rain. "Have you lost your mind, girl?"

"What about you?" I ask, ignoring his question. "I thought you said it was too dangerous to go out today."

"We're heading home," replies the other man, taking his pipe out of his mouth and thrusting it into his pocket. He grabs the edge of my skiff as it drifts toward him. "Got to get these dinghies out of the water before the brunt of the storm hits. Where's your father?"

"He went to the island. Caleb Hanlon took him."

"Fools, both of them," the white-haired man mutters, shaking his head.

"That's Mac Forester's dinghy you're sitting in," the other man informs me. "I suppose he knows you're using it?"

"I'm going," I say, avoiding the question. I pull the skiff toward the dock, tie it to a cleat, and scramble out.

"Where you off to, girl?" the older man asks, studying me with his faded blue eyes.

The moment he asks the question, I know. "I'll be all right," I say, heading off down the dock. "Thanks."

"Best get out of this rain," the man with the pipe calls after me. "You'll catch your death."

"Weather's coming," the white-haired man warns. "Heavy weather."

Their voices fade as I walk back across the parking lot to Maggie's, to the pay phone out front. I don't know if I'm trying to help Hugh or punish him, to save or destroy him. All I know is I that I'm finished standing back and letting my father make all the decisions. I'm through being ignored. For once I'm going to make things happen, whether Hugh likes it or not.

With trembling hands, I pick up the receiver and dial home.

Chapter 23

When I hear my mother's voice, my stomach tightens, but then I realize it's only the answering machine. "You've reached the Scully household," she says, sounding distant and tinny. "Please leave a message."

"Marianna," I blurt out, and then stop, not knowing where to begin, how much to tell. "It's me," I say at last. "Sienna. I'm in Teal Harbor. Hugh's going to the island. You've got to get up here right away. He's . . . he's . . ." My voice trails off. I can't bring myself to say he's planning to kill himself. It's information too intimate, too profound to speak into a machine.

"I'm going out there," I continue. "I'll stay with him until you get here. I'll take care of him. I'll—"

I hear a beep, and I know the tape has ended. I think of calling back, but what more is there to say? Instead, I hang up the phone and try to think. I've got to get out to the island, but how?

I'm still trying to figure it out when a tall man in yellow rain gear appears at the end of the dock. My breath catches in my throat as he walks toward the parking lot. It's Caleb!

"Caleb!" I call, running up to meet him. "I didn't think you'd be back. The other fishermen went home already."

"I should be doing the same," he replies, pushing his wet hair back from his forehead, "but I didn't feel comfortable leaving until I made sure you were all right. I don't know what's going on between you and your father—it's none of my business, really—but you looked plenty upset when we sailed away."

I hesitate, wondering what to tell him. "My father is sick," I say. "He thinks he can take care of himself, but he can't. I need to be with him."

"Best wait until tomorrow."

"But the men said the storm will be worse tomorrow."

"Maybe. Myself, I think it'll either hit tonight or hold off a bit. Maybe even change direction and head out to sea."

"I can't wait around to find out," I tell him. "I need to get out there now."

He looks me over, considers. "You've got the same look in eye as your father. You planning to steal a skiff and take off?"

"I already tried that," I admit. "I got lost and turned back."

"You're lucky you didn't capsize." He sighs and heads back down the dock. "Come on." I follow at a jog and watch as he climbs back into his skiff. He reaches under the seat and produces a plastic milk carton. "I'm probably crazy, but what the hell. Get in and start bailing."

"Thanks," I say gratefully, climbing in fast before he can change his mind. He starts the engine and we take off at full throttle, blasting through the breakers. I clutch the gunwale with one hand and bail with the other. The wind blows my wet hair straight back, and the rain and spray feel like a thousand pin pricks against my face.

I glance over my shoulder at Caleb. His eyes are focused, alert, but his body is relaxed and there's a hint of a smile on his lips. Unlike me, he knows exactly what he's doing.

Within minutes, a white wooden boat with black trim comes into view. The name of the boat, "Meredith," is painted in black letters across the stern. "There she is!" Caleb shouts.

He pulls up alongside, anchors the skiff, and climbs on board. I climb up after him. Caleb's boat is old, but clean and newly painted. A dozen lobster traps are stacked on the deck, along with coils of rope and a jumbled pile of black and yellow buoys. The smells of fish and diesel fuel hang in the air.

"There's another set of oilskins down below," Caleb says.

"What?"

"Rain gear. They'll be too big for you, but you can roll up the pant legs and sleeves. There are some dry clothes, too. Not too clean maybe, but you're welcome to them."

I walk to the wheelhouse and bow my head as I step down below deck. There are two bunks, neatly made, with a faded flannel shirt, a pair of stained jeans, and a gray sweatshirt lying on them. A pair of binoculars, a Boston Red Sox cap, and the yellow rain gear hang from hooks on the wall.

I take off my backpack and my wet shirt and pull the sweatshirt over my head. It's too big and it smells of fish and sweat, but it's warm and dry and comfortable. I decide against the oilskin pants with their long suspenders, but I slip on the bulky jacket, roll up the sleeves, and flip the hood over my head.

Up on deck, Caleb has started the engine and is bringing up the anchor. "Now you look like you belong here," he says with a smile. "I've half a mind to make you haul some traps."

"All right," I answer uncertainly, not quite sure if he's serious, or what hauling traps actually entails.

Caleb laughs. "Maybe some other time. Right now I don't want to spend any longer out here than I have to."

He walks to the wheel and puts the engine into gear. The boat takes off across the bay, rolling and pitching as the bow cuts through the waves. "Your father's an artist?" he asks over the drone of the engine.

I nod, but I'm not sure anymore. An artist creates. Hugh builds metal rooms with hefty price tags. "A sculptor," I say.

"My dad and I make a little extra cash ferrying tourists to and from the islands every summer. We've met a lot of artists."

I blush, suddenly realizing he must be expecting me to pay for this trip. "I . . . I'm sorry," I stammer. "I don't have much money. I'll have to ask my father when we get to the island."

He frowns at me, puzzled. Then he gets it and shakes his head. "This isn't about money," he says. "I mean, that's not why I'm taking you out to Birch Cove. It's because . . . I don't know. I can tell when someone's hurting. I've been there myself."

I look away, alarmed to realize he can read my feelings. But at the same time, it's a relief to be found out. "I haven't had much sleep lately," I say. It isn't exactly a major revelation, but for me it's a lot to admit, especially to a stranger. Only somehow Caleb doesn't seem like a stranger.

"You said your father is sick," he says. "Is it serious?"

I consider lying, but I know Caleb can read the answer on my face, so I just nod and say, "He's dying." The words catch in my throat and I have to press my lips together to keep them from trembling.

Caleb sees what's happening and starts talking, his voice low and soothing. "My father is a lobsterman. My grandfather, too. They taught me about the ocean, but my mother taught me other things—about books, music, the world outside of Teal Harbor. After she died—I was ten at the time—I decided I wasn't going to be a fisherman. I was going to go to college, move to the city, maybe write or teach. I did it, too—for a while, anyway. Started junior college in Boston, but I couldn't take it. The city didn't smell right. The sidewalks were too solid, too stationery, and you had to look up between the skyscrapers to see the seagulls."

"So you came back?"

He nods. "I worked for my dad until I had enough money to put a down payment on this boat. I christened her *Meredith*. That was my mother's name."

I look into his eyes. They're chestnut brown. His eyelashes are long and damp and he has a tiny, crescent-shaped scar beside his left eyelid. "Then you've decided," I say. "You're going to be a lobsterman like your father and grandfather."

He shrugs, then pauses to steer the boat through a gust of wind strong enough to tip her over. There's a pulley on the starboard side for hauling lobster traps. I grab hold of it and struggle to stay standing. When finally we hit a patch of calmer seas, he turns to me. "If I want to write, I can do it right here, can't I? I don't need to move to Boston."

He smiles and I smile back, grateful that Caleb knew I didn't want to break down in front of him, that he knew how to take me out of myself until the moment passed, until I'm in control again.

"There's Birch Cove," he says, pointing off the port bow.

I see a gray smudge on the horizon, flat and low on one end, high and craggy on the other. I know every inch of the island, every spruce and fir, every rock and tide pool. Even now, I can almost smell the tang of balsam and feel the tickle of salt hay against my legs as I walk down to the sea.

"Your family owns the place?" Caleb asks.

"Yes. I've been coming here every summer since I was born."

"I've got my own island," he says, then chuckles. "Truth be told, nobody owns it, least not as far as I know. It's just a hunk of rock with a few spruce trees on it. I built a little dock on the leeward side. I go there sometimes, just to be alone."

"You're not alone on your boat?" I ask.

"It's different. When I'm on the boat, I'm working. On the island, I just sit and think."

We're coming up on Birch Cove now. I can see the spruce trees, tall and black against the sky, the birches along the shore, and our old wooden cabin standing among them. Waves are crashing against the granite boulders at the southern tip of the island, but in the tiny, protected harbor in the middle of the crescent-shaped cove, the water is relatively calm.

Caleb moors the *Meredith* outside the harbor. There's a small orange pontoon boat tied up in the boat's stern. I retrieve my backpack from below deck while he lowers the boat into the choppy water. Then we climb in.

"I'm impressed," he says as he starts the engine. "I thought by now you'd be pea green and puking your guts out."

I laugh, then gasp as a wave crashes over the left pontoon. "Let's go," I gulp.

He opens the throttle and we roar across the water to the dock. I climb out, and the moment my feet touch the island, my thoughts turn from Caleb to Hugh. Is he in the cabin? Is he alive?

"Do you want to come ashore?" I ask Caleb, but I know my voice is less than inviting. I don't mean to seem ungrateful, but I don't want him here now. No matter what's in store for me, I have to face it alone.

Caleb understands. "I'd best be getting back," he says.

"I'll stop by tomorrow, weather permitting, to see how you're doing." There's a chipped yellow and black buoy in the bottom of the pontoon boat. "If you don't want to see me, tie this to the piling. I'll keep on going."

He hands it to me, then puts the engine in reverse and chugs away from the dock. I hug the buoy to my chest and watch as he returns to the lobster boat, climbs in, and pulls the pontoon boat up after him. Soon the *Meredith* begins to move, and within thirty seconds I've lost sight of her in the wind and the waves and the rain. Caleb is gone.

Chapter 24

I drop the buoy on the dock and turn my back on the ocean, my face to the trees. Then I head up the path toward the cabin.

Damp pine needles cushion my feet. The only sounds are the raindrops hitting the canopy of the spruce trees, the wind rustling the dead leaves of the birches, and the distant crash of the ocean against the rocks. Birch Cove Island is only half a mile long, less than half that across, but when I'm there, it becomes my whole world. Maybe that's why despite everything that's happened, everything that awaits me, I feel a quiet calm growing inside me, a stillness that makes me strong.

At the cabin door, I pause. The padlock is open, but there's no smoke coming from the chimney, no sound from inside. What will I find when I open the door? My brain shuts down, refusing to supply any grisly images, but my heart is pounding and my stomach is churning like the sea. Ignoring them, I take a deep breath and open the door.

The curtains are drawn and the room is so dark it takes a few seconds for my eyes to adjust. But Hugh sees me. "What are you doing here?" he growls. "I told you to go home."

His words reignite my anger. "I'm not a child," I say, walking toward the chair where he sits wrapped in a quilt, a half-empty bottle of whiskey resting between his legs. "I can do as I please."

"I don't want you here, Sienna. Don't you understand? This doesn't concern you."

"You told me that once before," I remind him, "when I caught you kissing Evelyn Fadulo. You'd like to believe it, too, wouldn't you? That nothing you do affects me, that it doesn't matter. Then you could slit your wrists with a clean conscience."

I don't know what makes me so bold. I've never talked to Hugh like that before, never even wanted to. But now I couldn't keep my mouth shut if I tried. Maybe it's because I figure this is my last chance. Because I've got nothing to lose.

"What the hell do you want from me?" he asks wearily.

"Nothing," I snap. "Why should I want anything from my father?"

"That's enough, Sienna. There's no need to be sarcastic." He tips his head back, takes a long swig of whiskey. "Take off that raincoat and sit down. Then we'll figure out how to get you back to the mainland."

I shake my head and stand my ground. "Didn't you hear what I said? I'm not going back."

He smiles indulgently, as if I were a naughty toddler who refused to go to bed. "Sit down, Sienna."

"No!"

He stares at me, startled, then suddenly he reaches out and grabs the sleeve of my raincoat. "Damn it," he barks, pushing me toward the chair, "I said sit!"

There's something about the feel of his hand on my arm

that makes me explode. Without thinking, I whip my sleeve out of his grasp and now I'm hitting him, my fists flailing against his head, his neck, his shoulders. He tries to grab my wrists, but I'm too strong for him, and much too fast. "I hate you!" I scream, pummeling him again and again. "Do you understand? I hate you!"

The bottle of whiskey falls to the floor, but I don't care. I'm too furious, too out of control. Until gradually I realize he's not fighting back anymore. He's balled up against the side of the chair, arms over his head, cowering.

I stop now, exhausted, and for the first time since I entered the cabin, I take a close look at Hugh. His hair is damp and disheveled. His clothes are wet, his teeth are chattering. He looks old and sick and frail.

"Why didn't you start a fire?" I ask.

He lowers his arms and raises his head to look at me. "I . . . I couldn't find the matches."

"Take those wet clothes off," I tell him. "I'll get something dry for you to put on." I slip off my backpack and Caleb's raincoat and hang them on the doorknob. Then I go into the bedroom and rummage through the dresser. There are no socks or underwear, but I find a pair of black sweatpants, a T-shirt, and a moth-eaten black sweater.

When I walk back into the living room, Hugh is stripping off his soggy pants. His legs look white and clammy, and as he tries to pull his pant legs over his shoes, he loses his balance and pitches forward onto the floor. I rush over to him, lean down and help him sit up. That's when I realize he's crying.

The sight chills me. He looks like an oversized little boy, helpless and pathetic. I feel like crying myself, but instead I untie his shoes, take them off, and pull off his pants. Then I help him into the sweatpants. I get the T-shirt and sweater on him, and lead him back to the chair. He's not crying now; he's just staring at the floor with vacant, half-closed eyes.

I wrap the quilt around his shoulders and go about starting a fire. There's dry wood stacked by the stove. The matches are where they always are, in the box on the wall. It's a small thing, but it makes me realize—maybe more than anything else that's happened on this trip—that it's not just Hugh's body that's failing him. His mind is going, too.

I put three logs in the stove, add some crumpled sheets of newspaper, and light them. I leave the stove door open so the room will heat up faster. Then I glance over at Hugh. He's gazing at the fire now, his eyes still at half-mast.

I go into the bedroom and exchange my wet jeans for some dry ones. Back in the main room, the damp air is warming up. Hugh's stopped shivering and his shoulders are relaxed. I sit in the chair beside him and together we watch the fire. The only sounds are the crackle of the flames and the patter of the rain against the windows.

"I didn't plan on kids," he says softly. "You were an accident, but Marianna wanted to go through with it, so we did."

I turn to him, startled to hear that Marianna is the one who wanted me, hurt to learn that Hugh didn't. He glances at me and sees the pain on my face.

"The first time I saw you," he tells me, "everything changed. I held you in my arms and I knew I loved you."

I gaze at him skeptically.

"It's true," he says. "Don't you believe me, Sienna?"

"No," I answer.

He lets out a long sigh, runs his hand though his damp hair. "When you were born, I promised myself I'd be a better father than mine had been. But how? I didn't know anything about dealing with a daughter. I still don't. I always feel you *want* something from me, but I don't know what it is. And then I see you watching me, judging me. Blaming me for not knowing what you need."

"If I've been holding back, watching you," I cry, my words tumbling out in a rush, "it's because I never know how to act around you. All I want—all I've ever wanted— is to mean something to you, to make you pay attention to me, to make you care. But you're always so busy with your work, with *important* things. How can I compete with that?"

"Sienna, it's not that simple. I—"

But I cut him off with a wave of my hand. "When you asked me to bring you here, I thought maybe I finally had a chance. If I could do something that mattered to you, then maybe you would think I mattered, too." I shake my head. "But that was just wishful thinking. It isn't going to happen, not now, not ever."

"What do you mean?" he asks with a frown. "What you did for me matters more than I can say. I couldn't have made it up here without your help."

"Oh, come on," I snap, indignant that after everything that's happened, he's got the nerve to pretend he really cares about me. "You didn't need *me*. You just needed a driver to take you from point A to point B. Any warm body would have sufficed."

"That's right," he says. "I could have asked anybody. But I didn't. I wanted *you*."

"Oh, I get it. You knew how desperate I was to be with you, so you figured I wouldn't give you any trouble?"

"No, that's not it. I—"

" 'I know,' " I say, mimicking his voice, " 'I'll get Sienna to drive me. She'll take any kind of crap I hand her, then sit up and beg for more.' "

"Stop it!" Hugh cries. "Just stop! I'd never use you like that. I never used anyone in my life. You should know that about me by now. When I don't know how to deal with something—or someone—I just retreat. I get drunk, or go into my studio and lose myself in my art. I'm not clever enough to manipulate people."

Is that true? I wonder. I have my father pegged as a self-centered user, doing whatever it takes to feed his ego. But maybe his actions aren't as self-conscious, as well thought-out as I'd imagined. Maybe he's just running scared, making up his life as he goes along.

"So what are you saying?" I ask sarcastically. "That you wanted me to come up here with you so we could spend some quality time together?"

He laughs ruefully. "You aren't going to let me off easy, are you, Sienna?"

I look him in the eye, shake my head.

"All right," he says, "I'll admit I asked you to come with me because I knew you wouldn't try to talk me out of it, because I was confident you wouldn't turn around and call Marianna the first time things got a little rough."

I look away so Hugh won't see the guilt on my face. Then I remind myself that what I've done is best for everybody, Hugh included. Only helping Hugh wasn't my motivation for calling Marianna. I wanted to get back at him, thwart his plans. I wanted to hurt him as much as he hurt me.

If Hugh knows what I'm thinking, he doesn't show it. "But there was another reason I wanted you along on this trip, Sienna," he continues. "A much more compelling one."

"What do you mean?"

He hesitates, trying to find the right works. "It started the first time Marianna went to L.A.," he says slowly. "I had this thing growing inside my head and I was scared. Marianna was telling me I was getting better, but I didn't feel better. And there you were, skulking through the house with those big, dark eyes of yours. So I took a chance and reached out to you."

I look at him, wondering if I dare believe him. "It felt good," I admit.

He nods. "To me, too. Then I found out I was dying,

and I realized this trip was probably my last opportunity to get to know you. My last chance to understand what being a father is all about."

At first, his words sound so sentimental, so unlike anything I've ever heard Hugh Scully say, that I almost burst out laughing. But despite my cynicism, there are tears in the corners of my eyes. Despite everything I've been through, I still desperately want to believe.

It's then that a new slide show begins flashing inside my head. I see my father and me standing side by side in front of the Kandinskys, sharing the moment, lost in the color and the shape and the line. I see us eating together, laughing, talking, and I think about the things he's told me over the last few days, the secrets he's revealed. It couldn't have been easy for Hugh to admit that he wasn't able to paint as well as he wanted to, that he switched to sculpture because it didn't involve his heart and soul, that he chose to be rich and bored instead of hungry and honest and real.

And then it occurs to me that maybe by sharing these things, Hugh was trying to reach out to me. Maybe that was the only way he could think of. The only way he knew to be a father.

The fury I felt has dissipated, like rain seeping into dry earth. In its place is emptiness, waiting to be filled. "Are you hungry?" I ask.

Hugh looks at me a long time, then nods. "I can't remember the last time I ate."

"Let's see what we've got." I walk to the pantry and open the door. There's some instant coffee on the shelf, three boxes of pasta, a dozen cans of tuna fish and soup. I reach for a pot and set about making us some lunch.

Chapter 25

The smell of clam chowder fills the cabin. I pour the thick, hot liquid into a bowl and hand it to Hugh. He takes it, but he can't make his left hand pick up the spoon.

"Here," I say, perching on the arm of his chair and holding the bowl so he can use the spoon with his right hand. He sips, dribbling a few drops down his chin. I don't want to see it, don't want to be reminded how much coordination and control he's lost. So I quickly wipe the drips away with a towel and say, "You can't kill yourself, Hugh."

"Give me one good reason why not."

"Because you have art to create," I answer, surprised to find myself parroting Marianna's line. "People are touched by what you do. You owe it to them to keep working as long as you possibly can."

"And that's what counts?" he asks. "The fact that people are moved by my art? But what if the art is a pile of crap?

What if the man who creates it is just going through the motions? Or isn't that important?"

"Your installations aren't crap," I tell him, and I mean it. "They make people see the world in a new way. They did that for me."

He gazes up at me and the hard look in his eyes slowly softens. "If they did that for you, then they're not crap. I certainly didn't view them that way when I started. But it's been—what?—over fifteen years now, and I haven't moved forward. I've become a technician instead of an artist."

"But what about the new one?" I ask. "The forest. That's a step forward."

He shakes his head wearily. "I was desperate to make a change, a *real* change, but I didn't know how. In any case, I didn't have the courage. I knew Marianna wouldn't approve, and Evelyn would worry I was going in a new direction that wouldn't sell. So I switched from bronze furniture to bronze trees, knowing damn well it was enough of a departure to interest the critics but not enough to alienate the collectors."

I think back to the evening we ate pasta in the studio together, the evening he showed me the trees. "If the installation meant so little to you, why did you bother asking me if I thought you could get away with a scaled-down version?" I ask. "Why didn't you just do it?"

"Because I cared about your opinion. It was a good one, too. I envisioned a life-sized forest, and that's what I needed to create."

"But you stopped working on it," I point out. "And at the opening you told Evelyn not to show or sell any of your new work."

He nods. "When I found out I was dying—not just suspected it, but *knew* it—that's when I realized I couldn't go on repeating myself. The problem is, now that I know I can't go back, I've been denied the possibility of moving on." He lets out a hollow laugh. "Ironic, isn't it?"

"But there's still time," I insist, desperately wanting to

believe it. "You can start over, make art you really care about, art that truly matters—not to Marianna, or Evelyn Fadulo, or some critic, but to *you*."

He doesn't respond, and I think he must be spacing out again. Then he sits back in the chair and says, "There have been moments when I wanted to set my studio on fire and walk away. Maybe head into the woods with a pencil and a pad of paper, like you."

The thought that Hugh has considered creating art that in any way resembles mine completely floors me. But then I remind myself that any sketches Hugh might do would be so totally different from mine, so vastly superior, that they wouldn't even be in the same universe. Finally, all I manage to say is, "You don't want to paint again?"

"My installations are monochromatic. That's part of what makes them easy for me. But to work in color . . ." He hesitates. "Color is a beast you have to capture and tame. It frightens me."

I think of my little black-and-white sketches, my fear of color, and it shocks me to realize that for the second time in five minutes Hugh has compared himself—knowingly or unknowingly—to me. "But if you could find a way to combine painting and sculpture . . ."

"Now that would be something worth doing," he agrees.

"Then do it. What are you waiting for?"

"It's not that easy, Sienna. I'm so weak, so tired."

"You have to fight it," I insist, echoing my mother again. "You can't give in to your illness. You can't—"

"Damn it!" he shouts, flinging out his hand and sending the soup bowl flying. "Don't you think I wish it were that simple?" He staggers to his feet, hurls the spoon down, too. "Look at me!" he cries. "I've been fighting so hard I'm exhausted. Don't you understand, Sienna? I don't want to fight anymore. I want to lie down and rest. I want to *die*."

I stare at the bowl, shattered on the faded Navajo throw rug. Then I look at him. The shock on my face must be obvious because he lowers himself heavily, awkwardly onto one knee and reaches out to take my hand.

"Sienna, listen to me," he says and his voice is urgent, insistent. "I asked the doctor in Philadelphia to tell me the truth, no matter how painful, and he did. The headaches and seizures are only going to get worse. I can take drugs to control them, but then I'll be in a constant stupor, the way I was last night after I left the hospital. Either way, I'm going to have more and more trouble walking, talking, using my hands. I'll lose control of my bladder and my bowels. But the worst part is, my mind is going to go. I won't be *me* anymore. I'll be a vegetable, a non-person, until finally my brain shuts down completely and I die." He closes his other hand over mine, squeezes it tight. "It might take a month, Sienna, it might take a year. But it *is* going to happen."

Up until that moment, I guess there was always a part of me that believed Hugh was going to get better. In the beginning, back at the farmhouse, it was because Marianna said he was—and I believed her unconditionally. But later, even after Hugh told me the truth, after I watched his body deteriorate and heard him vow to end his own life, I still didn't want to face it. Maybe it was because I simply couldn't imagine life without my father. Or because my image of Hugh had already been so tarnished, so damaged, that I was desperate to hold on to something I could believe in. And so I convinced myself that even if his character was weak, his body was still strong, still invincible.

But now, gazing into my father's unshaven face, his chin stained with chowder, his eyes moist and his lips dry and cracked, I know he's going to die. And I'm filled with a tremendous sense of relief because now, after so many weeks, I can let down my guard and finally welcome the sadness. It comes like floodwaters, sweeping me away, drowning me. I'm weeping now, swooning against my father's chest as all my strength, all my resistance, is washed away. And despite the tears, I'm smiling because holding it in hurt so much, and because I know I don't have to anymore. The charade is over, over for good.

"Sienna, don't cry," Hugh says, moving his hands helplessly in midair. I know he wants to comfort me but he doesn't know how.

"It's all right," I sob. "It's all right."

"Maybe you should lie down," he suggests uncertainly. I don't resist, so half-stumbling, left foot dragging, he leads me into the bedroom, and I don't know which one of us is in worse shape, him or me. But I don't care. I'm just so glad to be crying, to feel my sorrow so intensely, to stop holding back and simply be.

The bed is soft and I bury my head gratefully into the musty pillow. I think I might cry for days, for weeks, forever.

Hugh is hovering over me, waiting for some sign, some indication of what he should do. I want him to hold me, to cradle me like an infant, to make up for all the years he never touched me at all. But I can't bring myself to ask him, and I know he can't do it on his own. Maybe he'll never be able to.

"I'm tired," I say, letting him off the hook. "I just need to rest a while."

Hugh nods eagerly, gratefully. "Perhaps I'll open up the studio," he murmurs, more to himself than me. The studio is actually a shed out back behind the cabin. When he's on the island, Hugh works in clay, creating preliminary models of his future installations.

He turns now, not waiting for an answer, and suddenly it occurs to me that he might be planning to end his life, right here, right now. "You won't—?" I cry, reaching out for him.

I can't seem to finish the sentence, but Hugh understands. "Not now," he says softly. "Not today. I'm not ready yet."

Then he's gone, and I let the tears come, uncontrolled, inconsolable, until eventually, I drift off to sleep.

Chapter 26

When I wake up, my tears have stopped and so has the rain. I get up and walk to the window, rubbing my swollen eyes as I gaze into the fading afternoon light. Dripping spruce boughs sway in the wind, and somewhere among the birches, a chickadee trumpets its two-note refrain.

Caleb was right, I tell myself. *The storm either held off or changed direction.*

I feel inexplicably elated and suddenly I know I have to get out of this cabin, I have to smell the wet earth, hear the seagulls, touch the sea. It's been hours and hours since I sketched anything and I feel like an addict, shaky, excited, and desperately eager.

I hurry through the main room of the cabin, ignoring the broken bowl still lying on the floor, and go outside, grabbing my sketchbook from my backpack. I pull a bucket of water up from the well and splash my face, then walk around back to the shed. I can see Hugh in the window, hunched over, concentrating on something. I consider checking on him, making sure he's all right, but I don't want to disturb him. Besides, my hands are twitching, alive with nervous energy. I need to draw.

I follow the path to the northern tip of the island, where a wide, rocky ledge juts into the ocean and tidepools fill every dip and crack. The ocean has turned from gray to green, the wind is dying down. I walk out across the granite ledge, slipping on rockweed and algae, and pause to watch a group of cormorants diving for their dinner. At my feet a tidepool crowded with sea urchins, periwinkles, and starfish catches my eye. I open my sketchbook and start to draw.

The sky is a heavy blanket of clouds, and the colors, robbed of shadow and glare, are intense. As always, they overwhelm me and I long for the courage, the power to put them down on paper. But I don't have it, not yet. So I concentrate on the shapes and textures—the pliant skin of the starfish, the urchins' thorny spines.

An hour later, I'm still drawing, oblivious to the growing darkness, the cold, lost in the sound of the ocean and the beauty of the tidepool at my feet. Then suddenly, I hear my name and feel a warm hand on my shoulder. I spin around to find Hugh standing over me.

"How long have you been there?" I ask, quickly closing the sketchbook and scrambling to my feet.

"Don't," he says, reaching out to take the book from my hands. My heart slams against my ribs. I hold my breath. He opens it and slowly, silently turns the pages.

"Marianna thinks I can be a decent illustrator someday," I say, laughing at myself before he can laugh at me.

But Hugh isn't even smiling. "You can be an artist if you want to." He looks me in the eye. "Do you, Sienna?"

"I . . . I don't know."

"Look here," he says, suddenly frowning. He holds up a sketch of tulips in a vase beside the kitchen sink, the one I drew while I was waiting for the ambulance to arrive on the morning of his first seizure. "You're too tight, too technical. You've got to loosen up, feel it." He swings his right arm, drawing imaginary pictures in the air. "Look at you," he barks suddenly. "You hold your body like you hold a pencil. Anyone would think you're about to snap!"

It's the old Hugh again, and I feel like four-year-old Sienna in my father's studio, hanging my head as he passes judgment on my little crayon scribbles. Or is it fifteen-year-old Sienna, cowering behind the barn door. His voice echoes inside my head: "You're probably still a virgin."

Hugh flings his arm out again and I wince, involuntarily lifting a hand to protect my face. He stops and turns to me, a puzzled frown on his face. "What's the matter?" he asks.

"I remember the last time you accused me of being too uptight," I say. "I wanted to please you, to make you approve of me. So I picked the first guy who paid attention to me and practically handed myself to him on a platter. It didn't quite come off, but I did learn that sex for the sake of sex doesn't feel very good." I look away, then turn back and blurt out, "You might want to consider that the next time you get the urge to cheat on Marianna."

Hugh's mouth falls open and he stares at me, dumbfounded. I've gotten to him, I can see that, and it feels good. "I . . . I was just trying to shake you up," he says at last. "I didn't mean . . ."

"What about Marianna?" I break in. "Are you trying to shake her up, too?"

"Something like that." He lets out a sigh, gazes across the water at the orange sunset. "I don't suppose you'll believe this, but we do love each other."

I kneel down, dip my fingers in the tidepool. "I used to think the bond between the two of you was so strong, so tight, there was no room for me."

"That's a good analogy. Our love is like a knot—complex and twisted. Maybe that's why we were attracted to each other in the first place. We each had something the other person couldn't live without. How healthy that is, I don't know."

"What do you mean?"

He smiles faintly. "Marianna is my father and mother, all rolled into one. She bullies and babies me. We have a sort of unspoken understanding. I give her what she wants—to be the wife and business manager of a world-renowned artist—and in return, she condones my little escapades."

I turn to him, startled. "You mean she knows you cheat on her?"

He snorts a laugh. "Knows? The first time, she practically arranged it."

"But why?" I ask incredulously. "I mean, doesn't she care?"

"She cares," he says. He picks up a shell and tries to skip it across the water. It bounces off the ledge and sinks into the sea. "Marianna knows me better than I know myself. When I can't handle things, when I feel like a hypocrite or a failure, I retreat. I drink, I ignore my only child, I make love with other women. Marianna puts up with it—uses it, even—to get what she wants."

I don't say anything. What is there to say? There's more to my parents' relationship than I'll ever know, more than I can possibly understand. All I know for sure is that there's no clear villain, no obvious victim. Their marriage is an intimate pas de deux, full of pain and pleasure, love and hate.

"The truth?" Hugh asks, and he's not talking about Marianna now. He's leafing through my sketchbook. "You've got talent—plenty of it." He turns to my drawing of the wren hopping among the chrysanthemums. "Look at these flowers. The detail, the shading. They're exquisite."

My heart is soaring and I have to swallow hard to keep from crying. "Thank you," I murmur.

He smiles—or at least I think he does. It's getting too dark to see clearly. "It's cold," he says. "Let's go back."

At the cabin, I put more logs on the fire, light the kerosene lanterns, finally clean up the broken bowl and spilled chowder. Hugh pulls a chair near the stove and warms his hands. His shoulders are slumped and he looks tired. I cook pasta with tomato sauce and we sit at the unfinished pine table, the one Hugh built by hand last summer.

"I saw you in the studio," I say. "Are you working on something?"

He shakes his head. "I was looking at my paints. I opened each tube and squeezed out a dab of color. I'd forgotten how beautiful they are."

"You have paints here?" I ask with surprise.

He nods. "I did some of my best work on the island. That was long ago, before you were born."

I picture him young and healthy, sitting at his easel by the water's edge. Marianna is nearby, her slacks rolled up to her knees, wading in the surf. "You were happy then," I say.

He gazes into the distance, but the scene he remembers is different from mine. "I don't know if I was ever happy," he replies, then pauses, considering. "Maybe now, now that I've stopped struggling." He smiles. "Another irony, I suppose."

He gets up from the table and takes my sketchbook from the coffee table where I tossed it. Sitting by the fire, he turns the pages. "There are no people in your drawings," he says. "Why?"

"People are hard," I begin, searching for the words. But how can I explain my feelings when I barely understand them myself? Finally, all I manage to say is, "Colors are hard, too. I'm like you, I guess. They overwhelm me."

"Of course people are hard," he shoots back. "I'm not talking about the physical act of reproducing the human form on paper—anyone can be taught to do that. But drawing people—really capturing their energy, their spirit—that involves opening up to them, letting them in, making yourself vulnerable. It's scary as hell."

"So how do you do it?" I ask.

"I don't. Have you ever seen a human being in one of my installations?"

I shake my head. "But—"

"Don't follow me," he warns, cutting me off. "The road I took will lead you away from feelings, from life. Let yourself experience the world. I don't mean empty sex, or drinking just to get high. I'm talking about allowing yourself to care, to hurt, to *feel*. Then go back to your art and dive into it. Use every shade of color you can mix, draw every object that excites you, every person who moves you, every emotion that matters."

He stands up and throws my sketchbook down in front of me. "Draw me," he commands.

"What?"

"Don't think. Just pick up a pencil and do it."

My fingers are trembling as I open the sketchbook and take out the pencil I left between the pages. Hugh sits back down in front of the fire. I look at him, but I'm too self-conscious to really pay attention. All I can think about is the fact that he's watching me, waiting to see what I can do, and I feel certain I'm going to disappoint him.

I close my eyes and take a deep breath, willing myself to relax. When I open them again, I force myself to look—really look—at Hugh. That's when I notice the dark circles under his eyes and the way his hair, uncut for weeks, brushes against his collar. I close my eyes again and when I open them I find myself marveling at the distinct U-shaped curve of his upper lip, so similar to mine. I remember watching those lips kiss Evelyn Fadulo, remember them grimacing in pain as I hit him again and again, picture them smiling at me as we stood on the rocky ledge at twilight.

And as I remember, I draw—losing myself in my father's face, in his spirit, his life. Now my hand relaxes, my pencil strokes become freer, and I realize I'm no longer standing back and analyzing the situation, no longer worrying or trying to second-guess myself. In fact, it seems I'm not thinking at all. I'm just doing, and it feels as if my hand and Hugh's face are one. I picture myself caressing his cheek, and a line appears on paper. It's as simple as that.

I don't know how long we sit there like that—maybe twenty minutes, maybe an hour—but eventually Hugh's eyes grow heavy and his head bobs against his chest. He's asleep now, but I'm still drawing, adding details, shadings, getting it right. Then finally, I know I'm finished.

The pencil falls from my hand, the fire fades to glowing embers, but still I don't get up. I'm watching my father, studying him, memorizing each wrinkle, each hair, making sure I never forget.

It's during that quiet moment, while he sleeps and I watch over him, that I finally realize the truth. Hugh Scully will never need me the way I need him, will never love me completely and unconditionally, will never be the parent I want him to be. And yet I know I love him—not for who I imagined he was, but for who he is.

Moving quietly, I get up and gently tuck a quilt around Hugh's shoulders. I add more wood to the fire, put out the lanterns, and walk into the bedroom. The rumpled bed looks warm and welcoming. So I take off my clothes, slip between the covers, and sleep.

Chapter 27

When I wake up, a dull gray light is shining through the window. The air is damp and the cold floor stings my feet. I pull on my clothes, teeth chattering, and hurry into the living room. The fire is out and Hugh's chair is empty.

A feeling of panic rises in my chest. I fling open the door and run outside. Through the trees I can see the early morning sky, blood red above the water. I jog around the cabin to the shed. Then I see it—Hugh's silhouette in the window, head bowed, intent.

I let out a lungful of air, then move closer, watching him and wondering how long he's been there, how he managed to light the kerosene lantern, if he's eaten. But most of all I wonder what he's doing. Is he still squeezing out dabs of paint, marveling at the smell, the texture, the vibrant colors? Or has he found the courage to pick up a brush and create something?

Despite my curiosity, I don't knock on the door, don't

call out his name or peer through the window. Somehow I know that what Hugh needs now is privacy. So I walk back to the cabin, wash my face in the frigid well water, and go inside to make myself some coffee.

My sketchbook lies closed on the table, just the way I left it, and I wonder if Hugh looked at his portrait when he woke up. As for me, I don't need to. I can still see every line, every shadow, still feel every caress. Gulping down my coffee, I grab my sketchbook and walk down to the dock to wait for Caleb.

The yellow and black buoy is lying where I left it. I toss it into the dead grass and take a seat on the edge of the dock. The wind is coming up, the gray-green water is rippled with whitecaps. I open my sketchbook and draw the dock, the sea, a flock of eiders flying low over the water, a cormorant diving into the foam.

Later, much later, I spot a white lobster boat on the horizon. I jump to my feet and wave my arms, not certain if it's really Caleb, or if he can see me even if it is, but too excited to sit still and wait. And I ask myself why the sight of Caleb's boat makes my heart skip and my mouth go dry.

The obvious answer is because he's a young man, good-looking and kind, who was there when I needed him. But there's something more, a connection that defies logic. Maybe it's because Caleb loves the ocean and the islands, because he knows how it feels to lose a parent, because I suspect we both feel much more than we know how to say. I guess that's why I'm still wearing the sweatshirt he lent me, why the musky smell of it pleases me, and the feel of the baggy, too-long arms hanging over my wrists makes me feel safe.

The boat is coming closer and I see Caleb behind the wheel, waving back to me. Now that I know he can see me, I become more self-conscious, more subdued. I sit back down and swing my feet over the water, waiting, as he anchors the *Meredith* and chugs toward the dock in the little orange pontoon boat.

But my eagerness overcomes my shyness and soon I'm on my feet, smiling and calling, "You came back!"

He ties up the boat and steps out. He's wearing worn jeans and a jacket the color of spruce needles. Black rubber boots, but no oilskins. "I didn't see the buoy, just you, so I figured I was welcome," he says. "How's your dad?"

"Okay, I guess. He's in his studio."

"That's good, isn't it?"

I don't know the answer, but I nod, hoping he's right. "The storm passed, just like you said it would."

"Held off a bit, more likely. None of the men at Maggie's went out this morning. That's a pretty good sign there's more weather on the way." He glances up the path toward the cabin. "How are you set for firewood?"

"There's a stack of logs out back but they need to be split. I'm going to search the beach for driftwood later today."

Caleb puts his hands on his hips, surveys the shoreline. "I've always wanted to take a look around this island. Tell you what. I'll chop some wood for you if you give me a tour."

"All right." I pick up my sketchbook and we start up the path, side by side.

"I pass Birch Cove almost every day," he says. "I've got a sweet spot just north of here."

"A sweet spot?"

He nods. "Good kelp beds and plenty of lobsters. I always do well there."

"I don't know anything about lobstering," I admit.

"I don't know anything about art. It's always interested me, though. When I was a little kid, my parents were friendly with a painter over on Monhegan. He used to let me hang around his studio sometimes. I enjoyed that."

146

"What kind of paintings did he do?" I ask.

"Seascapes, mostly. He tried to show me a few things, but I never could get the hang of it. I'm better with words than images, I guess."

"I'm just the opposite," I say as we reach the cabin. "I'd rather draw than talk."

"I'd rather write than do either." He shrugs. "Where's that woodpile?"

We walk around the cabin to a stack of logs covered with a sheet of blue tarp. Caleb peels back the tarp and picks up the ax that's resting against the wood. Then he pushes up his sleeves and sets to work.

The noise of the ax blade against the logs sends a flock of crows cawing and flapping into the sky. I know Hugh's heard it, too, and I look toward the door of the shed, wondering if he'll come out. Then I see his face at the window, but before I can catch his eye, he turns away. And the peculiar thing is, I don't feel ignored or shut out the way I probably would have in the past. Because I know now that Hugh's life in the studio will always be more important than his life in the world, his life with me. That's just a fact, a given.

I turn back to Caleb, watch the muscles on his forearms as he lifts the ax, then brings it down fast and hard to split the wood. He notices me watching him and smiles. "Paul Bunyan I'm not."

I laugh and he joins in. He chops a half dozen logs, replaces the tarp, and says, "Let's get these inside before the rain starts up again."

Inside the cabin, I see him glance around, taking it all in. "Pretty primitive," I say.

"But nice. I like things simple."

"Sometimes I think I'd be happy to live here all year round. Some people would be bored, I guess, but not me. I'd spend my days reading, walking, creating . . ."

"Are you a sculptor, too?" he asks.

I'm no artist, I think. That's my usual line, but for once I don't say it. "I draw," I tell him. "Pencil sketches." My sketchbook is under my arm and I see his eyes fix on it. I'm not ready to show it to him, though, so I toss it on a chair, then hurry out the door and call over my shoulder, "Let's go for a walk."

We head over to the windward side of the island, to a little sand beach littered with rocks and mussel shells. A cold wind is blowing hard and steady; choppy waves break against the shore.

"Maybe I'm crazy, but I love it here," Caleb says. "Even with sand and spray blowing in my face and the temperature dropping faster than a lead sinker, I love it."

I smile. "My father's like me. He'd live here if he could."

"What about your mother?" Caleb asks. "You haven't mentioned her."

I haven't thought about her much, either, except in relationship to Hugh. But now it hits me that she's on her way here; in fact, she could show up at any moment. I try to imagine her striding onto the island, feeling scared and angry and hurt, but hiding it all behind a mask of cool control. I picture her shutting up the cabin, leading Hugh down to the dock, expecting me to follow behind them, docile and penitent. It's an unsettling thought and I push it out of my mind.

"She doesn't love the island the way we do," I tell Caleb. "My father says it's because she's been coming here all her life."

"She takes it for granted, I suppose."

"Or maybe she has some bad memories." I'm not thinking about her childhood now, but about her years with Hugh, about the women he's loved. Perhaps some of those women live up here. That would explain why Marianna is always looking for excuses to stay in Pennsylvania, to leave Hugh alone on the island.

"You look like *you're* having some bad memories," Caleb says, gently touching my sleeve.

"Not exactly," I reply, and I think I'm actually trying to explain it to myself. "It's just that I've been seeing a lot of things differently lately. It takes some getting used to."

He doesn't ask me to explain. He just nods and gazes out at the sea. When he turns back, there's a smile on his face. "Come on," he says, "I'll race you to the end of the beach."

He takes off, his boots crunching against the brittle mussel shells. I follow, laughing and panting. Soon the sand ends and the shoreline turns rocky. Caleb leaps onto a craggy peak. "Ever hike along these rocks to the point?" he asks, motioning toward the island's southern tip.

"No," I reply. "They're too steep and slippery. Anyway, there's a path just a few yards inland."

"Not the same," he replies with a grin. "Come on, let's give it a try."

He holds out his hand. I hesitate, then take it, and he pulls me up beside him. We start off across the uneven granite, slipping on the blue-green algae, splashing through the tidepools, laughing as we stumble into each other. The wind tangles our hair and the crashing waves fling cold spray into our faces, but we continue on, like explorers charting an untamed land.

After ten minutes, the landscape changes. The rocks are no longer side by side, one touching another, but spaced out, with two or three feet of wet sand in between. Undaunted, Caleb leaps from rock to rock like a long-legged mountain goat. I follow gamely, barely keeping my balance, and even tumbling into the mucky sand once or twice. But each time I fall, I find him smiling down at me, hand outstretched, ready to pull me back up.

Eventually, off in the distance, I spy the towering rock that marks the tip of the island. "Land ho!" I proclaim, laughing and pointing.

But Caleb isn't paying attention. He's standing at the edge of a granite slab, frowning down at the sand.

"What is it?" I ask, walking up to join him. I look down and my hand flies to my mouth. A gray spotted seal lies sprawled in the sand, its skin covered with red, angry-looking wounds. There's a huge bloody gash in its hindquarters, and its tail is nearly ripped off.

"Poor little guy," Caleb mutters. At the sound of his voice, the seal looks up and barks weakly.

"What happened to him?" I ask.

"Probably had a close encounter with a boat propeller. Or maybe he was attacked by a shark and managed to get away."

"We've got to get help," I say.

"Where? The nearest vet is a good ten miles across the bay. Anyway, this little guy is too far gone. The best thing we can do for him is put him out of his misery."

"Kill him?" I ask with alarm.

"Either that, or let him die on his own. But I wouldn't feel right leaving him to suffer. How about you?"

I look down at the seal, watch it writhe and grunt as it tries without success to move toward the water. "How do we do it?" I ask.

"I'll take care of it," he says, lifting his jacket. There's a leather sheath on his belt. He opens it and takes out a fishing knife, then jumps off the rock and leans over the seal.

I close my eyes. There's a sharp bark, then silence. When I open them, Caleb is beside me again, his arm around my shoulder, guiding me toward the trees. "Let's find the path," he says.

He starts walking and I follow him, but I'm not thinking about the path or about Caleb, or even about the wounded seal. I'm thinking about Marianna. She's coming to the island to get Hugh, to take charge of him. She's going to do whatever it takes to bring him back home, to get him back into the studio. No matter that he'll be in pain, that he'll be frustrated and unhappy, that eventually he'll be too sick and confused to even know what's going on. As long as he's alive, she'll have a purpose in life, a reason to keep going. As long as his heart is beating, she won't be alone.

"Caleb," I say, stopping in my tracks, "I need you to take me back to Teal Harbor."

"Now? But what about your father?"

"This *is* about my father. Please, I have to go. It's important."

Caleb doesn't ask any questions. He just looks me in the eye a moment, then sighs. "I've seen that look before," he says. "You're going to swim to Teal Harbor if you have to."

"Will you take me?" I ask. "Please?"

He nods. "Let's go."

So I turn and start up the path, in the lead this time, on my way to put things right, to honor my father's wishes. I just hope I'm not too late.

Chapter 28

When we reach the cabin, Caleb stops at the well for a drink. I walk around back to the shed. Hugh's profile is still visible in the window, head bowed, shoulders hunched.

I knock on the door and after a long time he opens it just enough to reveal his head and one shoulder. There are smudges of paint on his face, his shirt, his hair. His eyes aren't really there, aren't focused. I'm not even sure he recognizes me until he says, "What is it, Sienna?"

And suddenly, I don't want to leave him, not now, not ever. Because maybe if I stay with him every moment, if I make him food and draw him pictures and ask him questions about art, he won't kill himself. It's an irrational thought, of course, because the whole reason I'm going to the mainland is to stop Marianna from intervening, to allow Hugh to end his life when and how he chooses. But it's a feeling I can't shake, and when I finally open my mouth, all I can bring myself to say is, "How's it coming?"

He looks at me, finally making eye contact, and for a long time he doesn't say anything, just studies my face as if it were a rare Kandinsky. "Caleb's here?" he asks at last.

I nod. "He stopped by to make sure we're all right."

"Can he take you to Teal Harbor?"

"Why?" I ask, startled to hear Hugh suggesting exactly what I had in mind.

"You know that little art supply shop on Gull Street?" he asks.

"Sara's Studio," I say with a nod.

"I want you to go there and buy me a set of oils, two or three bristle brushes, and a couple of red sables. My wallet's in the cabin. Take some money with you, all right?"

I nod, suddenly light-headed, giddy. Because if Hugh needs more paints to finish whatever he's working on, then I know he'll be waiting for me when I return. I know he's not ready to die yet.

"I'll get them," I assure him. "I'll bring back some fresh fish for dinner, too. See you in a couple of hours, okay?"

His eyes are drifting and I know he's thinking about the studio, about getting back to work. I turn, letting him go, and then impulsively I look back over my shoulder and say, "Good-bye, Dad."

But the door is already closing, the creaking hinges drowning out my trembling voice, and I'm alone.

Inside the cabin, I find Caleb looking through a book of Eliot Porter photographs. I make tuna sandwiches for both of us and leave a third sandwich on the table for Hugh. Then I put my sketchbook in my backpack, slip on Caleb's raincoat, and together we head down to the dock.

The sky is growing black, the wind is whipping, and by the time we reach the *Meredith*, it's raining again. Caleb opens the throttle and we plow across the bay. His skiff is filled with water and I spend the trip to the mainland alternately bailing frantically and lunging for the gunwale so I don't fly overboard. When we finally reach the dock, I leap out, overjoyed to be on solid land again.

"Okay, we're here," Caleb says, climbing out after me. "Now what?"

"Now I make a phone call."

He stares at me, probably thinking I've lost my mind, but too polite to say it. "I'll be in Maggie's. Come find me when you're finished, okay?"

I nod and head off for the pay phone. I punch in the number of the farmhouse, then hold my breath and wait.

"Hello?"

"Liesel, it's Sienna. I need to talk to Marianna."

"Oh, Sienna, it's so good to hear your voice! I was out and I didn't get your message until last night, and then I couldn't get hold of Mrs. Scully until this morning. She was in New York looking for Mr. Scully."

"Give me her number. I have to talk to her right away."

"She's not there anymore. She left for the airport right after we talked. She said she was going to catch the first flight to Portland, then drive up to Teal Harbor."

"When is she supposed to arrive?"

"I'm not sure. Are you in Teal Harbor now?"

"No," I lie. "That's why I'm calling. Hugh decided not to go to the island after all. We're on the road, heading north."

"Oh, good heavens," Liesel moans. "How will I contact Mrs. Scully?"

"I don't know. Listen, if she calls, tell her we're not on the island. Tell her to stay where she is and wait. I'll call you back when we stop for the night."

"Sienna, where are you?" Liesel asks anxiously. "How is Mr. Scully? Is he all right?"

"He's okay. We're both okay. Tell Marianna not to worry." Before she can ask me any more questions, I hang up.

It's raining hard now, really pouring. I walk into Maggie's and join Caleb at his table. "My mother's driving up from Portland," I say. "I have to wait for her."

He puts down his coffee cup. "When will she be here?"

"I don't know. Soon."

Caleb frowns. "Maggie told me the Weather Service just issued a gale warning. If we don't start back to the island right now, we won't be going—not today anyhow."

I'm so focused on intercepting Marianna, Caleb's words don't sink in. "I've got to talk to her," I insist. "I've got to keep her away from Hugh."

Caleb doesn't respond, just sits there watching as I compulsively tap my fingernails against the table. I'm biting my lip so hard, I can taste blood. "You want to tell me what's going on?" he asks at last.

I look over at him, wary, unwilling. But when I meet his eyes, it's like sailing into a safe harbor, and I find myself saying, "I told you yesterday my father's dying. What I didn't tell you is that it's a brain tumor. Malignant and inoperable. He's come to Birch Cove to commit suicide."

I expect to see shock on his face, disapproval maybe, but it isn't there. So I take a breath and go on. "I called my mother yesterday morning and told her to get up here. I know she'll stop him, and yesterday I wanted her to."

"And today?" he asks.

"I'm going to tell her he's not on the island. I'm going to say he left me here and headed up the coast in a rented car."

Caleb stirs his coffee, thinking it over. "Is she flying?"

I nod. "Then driving up from Portland."

"The flights will probably be delayed because of the storm," he says. "It doesn't matter, though, because no one's going to take her out to Birch Cove today. Not in this weather."

"You don't know Marianna," I say. "She'll call the Coast Guard and tell them Hugh's dying, that he needs to be rescued—anything to get out to him. My only hope is to intercept her, to convince her Hugh isn't there."

But at the same time, I'm thinking, *Hugh's expecting me back. What if I get stuck here and don't show up?* I picture him wandering around the island looking for me, feeling scared and confused. Maybe having another seizure and hitting his head on a rock, or trying to light a fire in the stove and burning himself.

But is any of that likely? For all I know, he might spend the rest of the day in his studio, might even fall asleep there without giving me or my whereabouts a second thought. When he gets absorbed in his art, he's like that.

And then I think, *What if this is the night he kills himself? What if I never get to see him again, never say goodbye?* But then I remember the paints I'm supposed to buy at Sara's Studio. As long as he's waiting for them, as long as he's looking forward to something, I know he isn't thinking about ending his life.

"I'm going to wait for my mother," I tell Caleb. "Even if it means spending the night in Teal Harbor, I'm going to wait."

"I'll wait with you," he says.

"Why?" I ask, wanting it so much, but still too scared to trust him.

"What's the alternative? Sitting home and watching TV?" He pauses, then reaches out and covers my hand with his. "I like you, Sienna," he says softly. "I like the way you look with rain on your face and wind in your hair. I like the way you care about things so much but try not to show it. I know you won't be here for long, but while you are, I want to be with you."

I look down at his hand covering mine, feeling its warmth, its weight. I'm overwhelmed, grateful, but too embarrassed to do anything except breathe, "Thanks."

Caleb responds by pushing back his chair and standing up. "I'm going out to my boat to get her battened down for the storm. Don't want to lose her. I'll be back as soon as I'm able."

After Caleb leaves, I move to a window table so I can watch the parking lot. I order coffee, take out my sketchbook and draw the table, the window, the faded curtains with boat flags on them. I'm drawing to make the time pass, glancing from the paper to the parking lot and back again, trying not to think.

After a while I get the idea to call the airlines, to find out what flight Marianna took and when she might arrive, but I keep getting stuck on hold. I'm still standing at the pay phone when Caleb returns, dripping wet and eager for a cup of coffee.

I'm about to head back inside with him when I remember the paints and brushes I'm supposed to buy for Hugh. So I leave Caleb to watch for Marianna and hurry over to Sara's Studio, a combination frame store, art gallery, and art supply shop housed in a tiny storefront. Sara is closing up early—"Weather's coming, darlin'"—but she lets me in and I buy a set of twelve oils and an assortment of brushes, tucking them into my pants when I leave so they won't get wet.

Back at Maggie's, the lunch rush is over and the place has emptied out. Caleb and I sit by the window for the rest of the afternoon, drinking countless cups of coffee and listening to the weather report on the radio, but mostly just talking.

"Tell me about your mother," he says, as the sun goes down behind the clouds and Maggie comes around to refill the sugar bowls. "What's she like?"

"Strong, smart, competent. She always knows what she wants and how to get it."

"Sounds like you," he says with a smile.

"No," I protest. "We're total opposites."

"Come on, I don't believe it. After all, she's your mother. Your role model, right?"

It's odd, I suppose, but the idea that Marianna could be my role model, that I must be like her in some way, comes as a big shock to me. And for the first time in my life, it occurs to me that maybe we are a little alike. When she went out of town, I had no trouble taking over her role as Hugh's number-one support person, his nursemaid and cheerleader. I let him hurt me, ignore me, embarrass me just as he does Marianna. By the time he tried to leave me in Teal Harbor I had even learned how to thwart his plans when I felt the need to get back at him, to manipulate him to get what I wanted.

"I think we both have trouble with relationships," I say at last. "Or at least I used to. I hope I'm changing." I'm thinking of Caleb now, of how I forget to obsess about my shortcomings when I'm with him, of how his smile makes me feel like I'm floating instead of struggling just to keep my head above water.

I glance up at him, hoping to see that smile now, but he's gazing out the window with a troubled frown. I follow his gaze, half expecting to see Marianna trudging through the rain. Instead, I see sleet blowing sideways across the parking lot.

"That clinches it," he says. "We're not going back to the island today. We'd never make it if we tried."

"Maybe this is the worst of it," I say, unwilling to believe that I can't get back to Hugh now even if I wanted to, even if he needed me. "Maybe it'll let up soon."

He shakes his head. "I've lived here all my life, Sienna. I know the weather like I know my own mind. This storm will be blowing all night, you can count on it."

Caleb turns out to be right. The wind gets stronger, the sleet is so thick I can't make out the Range Rover on the other side of the parking lot. We stay in Maggie's until she closes, then we head out into the freezing darkness.

"Your mother must be stuck in Portland," Caleb says,

turning up the collar of his jacket. "Or maybe she never got out of New York." He looks at me. "I'm living with my father until I pay off my boat. You're welcome to spend the night."

The thought of laying my head down on a soft, warm pillow is almost irresistible, but I still can't convince myself that Marianna isn't going to show up, that she won't try to get out to Birch Cove tonight some way or other. At the same time, I can't stop thinking about Hugh. I picture him huddled inside the cabin, sleet blowing under the door, unable to start the fire, unable to remember where I've gone. I want to fly across the bay and comfort him, wrap the quilt over his shoulders and tell him everything is going to be all right.

"This parking lot is as close as I can get to my mother and father right now," I say, "and that's where I need to be. It's crazy, I guess, but I'm not going to leave."

To my surprise, Caleb doesn't try to argue with me. "Let's get in your car," he says simply. "We'll be warmer there."

I stare at him, not daring to believe I heard right. "You're staying with me?" I whisper.

"I told you I would. Come on."

He takes my hand and we head across the parking lot, stopping at his pickup truck to get an old wool blanket. At the Range Rover, I unlock the doors and we climb into the back seat. The windows are covered with sleet, and the wind is blowing so hard the doors are rattling. I'm tired, just totally drained, but I can't relax. I search under the seats, find a plastic snow scraper, then jump out to clean off the windows. By the time I climb back inside, they're almost covered again.

"Come here, Sienna," Caleb says, tapping the seat beside him.

I turn to him, one hand still on the door handle. "What?"

"Come here," he repeats, and his voice is gentle but insistent.

I move closer. He spreads the blanket across our legs, then slips his arm around my shoulder. "If your mother drives into the parking lot, we'll hear her."

"But—"

"Shh."

He guides my head toward his shoulder. I tell myself I have to keep the windows clear, I have to stay awake and keep watching, but it feels so good to lean against him, to feel my cheek against his fleece jacket and hear his steady breathing. So I stay there, breathing with him, until gradually the sound of my own breath seems to merge with his, soft and deep and steady. Until finally they both disappear into the white noise of the wind.

Chapter 29

I awake with a start, wondering where I am. Then I realize I'm lying across the back seat of the Range Rover, my head on my backpack, the wool blanket over my shoulders. "Caleb?" I cry, jumping up.

"I'm here," he says from the front seat. I can tell by the sound of his voice that I didn't wake him.

"What time is it?" I ask. Without waiting for his answer, I reach for the door. I have to push hard to open it, but when I do, I let out a gasp. The wind and sleet have stopped and the parking lot has disappeared under a blanket of snow.

"A little before six," he says. He glances out the door. "I didn't expect snow this early in the season."

But I'm not interested in the weather right now. "Why didn't you wake me up?" I demand. I jump out of the car and look around the parking lot. There are six or seven trucks and a couple of cars parked near the wharf. "Oh, my God, what if I missed her?"

Caleb gets out and comes around to join me. "Nobody's been in the lot all night except one cop. He shined his lights on us, then kept going. Those cars belong to Maggie and her cook, and the trucks to the local fishermen."

"You're sure?"

He nods. "I live here. I guess I know my neighbors by now."

I reach out and touch his shoulder, sorry that I shouted at him. "Thanks, Caleb."

He just smiles. "What now?"

I have to think a moment. "Call our housekeeper, I guess. Try to figure out where my mother is." I slosh across the parking lot to the pay phone. The snow is about three inches deep and wet.

I dial the farmhouse and Liesel answers. "Hello?"

"Did you hear from Marianna?" I ask.

"Oh, Sienna, thank goodness. I spoke to Mrs. Scully about an hour after you called. I told her you weren't on the island. She was absolutely frantic."

"Where is she now?"

"In New York, waiting to hear from you. Let me give you the number."

She tells me, but I don't have any way to write it down. It doesn't matter though. All I'm thinking about now is getting back to Hugh. "I have to go," I tell her.

"Sienna, is Mr. Scully there? Let me talk to him."

"He's getting gas. I'll call my mother when I know where we're staying."

"Sienna, wait! Where are you? Sienna, don't hang—"

I put down the receiver and hurry back to the car. "She's not coming," I tell Caleb. "Come on, let's get back to the island and make sure my father's all right."

We walk down to the docks. Caleb's skiff is still tied where he left it, but there's so much water in it that the bow is floating below the surface. We bail it out and climb in. After a dozen tries, the motor finally starts and we head out to the *Meredith*.

Caleb has lost some buoys and his VHF antenna is broken, but otherwise his boat is unharmed. He turns on the pump to clear out the water below deck, then we take off. A light wind is coming off the water and the swells are still high, but compared to yesterday Mussel Bay looks like a bathtub.

"Might be more weather on the way," Caleb says, gazing up at the gray sky, but I don't believe it. There are gulls and eiders everywhere, and we pass at least five fishing boats on our way across the bay.

Twenty minutes later, Birch Cove comes into view. I reach behind me to touch my backpack, thinking about the paints and the brushes inside, anticipating the pleased look on Hugh's face when I hand them to him. I try not to think about other options—that he might have spent the night looking for me, that he might be cold and scared and in pain.

Caleb anchors the *Meredith* offshore and we get into the pontoon boat. This is the first time I've seen the island after a snowstorm and it's beautiful. The rocks are capped with white, and wet snow hangs from the spruce boughs.

As we chug toward the dock, something catches my eye. There are small, dark shapes dotting the path leading up from the water. Caleb spots them a second later.

"What's all that?" he asks, pointing.

"I don't know." I blink and look again. Now I can see splotches of color in the snow—fuchsia and orchid, mustard yellow and teal green. I stare at them, baffled, until Caleb ties up the boat and I scramble out. I run across the dock to the path, then stop short and stare.

The objects sticking out of the snow are flowers. Not real ones, of course, but delicate wooden sculptures, painted with streaks and splashes of vibrant color that seem unnaturally bright against the pristine snow. I walk closer, entranced, and kneel down beside the closest one. The stem and leaves have been fashioned from slender peelings of spruce wood; the blossom is a crown of toothpick-thin wooden petals, painted burnt orange. It's an abstract version of a chrysanthemum, I realize. Like the ones growing around the farmhouse, the ones in my drawing of the wren.

I hear Caleb's footsteps behind me, but I don't turn, don't look up. I'm too absorbed in the shapes, the colors. I wander up the path, squatting beside each flower, marveling at it. "He did it," I breathe. "He found a way to combine painting and sculpture." What's more, he's created these intricate objects with one hand barely functioning, one eye half blind.

At the top of the hill I stop. The clearing in front of the cabin is scattered with carved wooden tulips, each one decorated with thick, multicolored brushstrokes of paint—eggplant purple, crimson, aquamarine. It's a joyous tableau, a celebration, and I ask myself how this can be the work of a dying man. These flowers speak of life, of hope.

It's then that I notice the cabin door is ajar. "Hugh!" I call, running up and flinging it open. "The flowers—they're beautiful!"

But the room is empty. There's snow on the floor, and the Eliot Porter book lies open, spine up, on the rug.

"Hugh?" I call, jogging into the back room.

He's not there so I hurry out to the shed and knock on the door. I'm so eager to see him, to congratulate him on finding the courage to paint again, to work in color. But there's no answer, so I knock again, then open the door and look inside.

Hugh isn't there. And then I notice the tubes of oil paints spread across the table. I step closer. There are dozens of them, none more than half empty. Beside them are eight or ten good brushes of different shapes and sizes.

"He didn't need the paints I bought," I say, trying to make sense of things, trying desperately to understand.

"He didn't need the brushes. He had everything he could possibly want right here."

My mind flashes to the flowers in the snow, so intricately carved and painted, so perfectly placed. It's a finished work of art, I'm sure of it. And suddenly I know my father is dead.

I turn from the table, feeling shaky and sick. Caleb is standing at the door of the shed.

"What's wrong?" he asks.

I don't answer, just push past him and take off, heart pounding and feet flying. Ignoring the path, I weave through the trees, calling Hugh's name, searching for some sign of him. When I reach the water, I turn and head along the shore, stumbling over rocks and fallen branches. I can't stop shouting my father's name; I can't stop hoping he'll answer. But the only sounds are the loud, slurred moan of an eider and the distant bellow of a boat horn.

So I keep running, dimly aware that Caleb is jogging along behind me, but too crazed to care. My lungs are burning and my throat is hoarse from shouting Hugh's name, but I keep going, following the curve of the island, until finally I come to the wide, rocky ledge at the northern tip, the place where Hugh watched me draw the tidepool.

And then I see it—a broken whiskey bottle shattered against the rocks and Hugh's black sweater lying wet and twisted nearby. I'm in shock, I guess, because I pick up the dripping sweater and carefully fold it. Then I spot something else lying out at the end of the ledge, near where the rocks disappear into the water. I sleepwalk toward it. It's one of Hugh's shoes. As I stoop to pick it up, I feel a hand on my shoulder.

I look around, half-expecting to see my father standing behind me. But it's Caleb. He slips his arms around me, whispers, "Sienna," and suddenly everything falls into place. Leaning against him, I close my eyes and picture my father carefully positioning the last painted flower in the snow. I see him hiking out to the ledge and polishing off the whiskey as the sun rises above the water. Then I see him throwing down his sweater and walking into the sea.

I open my eyes and it seems as if I'm looking at everything for the first time. The gray sky, the dark green ocean, the slippery black rocks beneath my feet—it's all so intense, so vivid, so breathtakingly beautiful. I'm still holding Hugh's sweater in my arms and now I press it to my cheek, comforted by the knowledge that my father ended his life exactly the way he wanted to—on Birch Cove Island, in this place, alone.

"Look," Caleb says quietly, "it's starting to snow again."

I lift my face to the sky. Fat, wet flakes are falling, melting as they touch my skin. I think about the wooden flowers, about how the snow will cover them, how the wind and the rain and the sun will ultimately destroy them. But I know it doesn't matter. They weren't created for the public. Hugh made them for himself. He made them for me.

The deep drone of a boat horn brings me back to the present, to the living. "Come on," I say, turning from Caleb, taking my first step back, "it's time for me to go."

Epilogue

I close my sketchbook and look around, letting my mind drift slowly back to the studio, back to now. The shadows on the barn floor have lengthened; the sun shining through the windows gives off a golden glow.

I stand up and stretch, and as I do, I think about my father, and about the portrait I drew of him. Looking at it again today, I was struck by how thin he'd become, how fragile. But beneath the illness, there was a serenity and an inner strength he'd never possessed before. I like to think I had something to do with helping him find that strength, that perhaps by demanding his attention, his respect, I showed him how to respect himself as well.

I think about Caleb, about how kind he was to me. I miss the feel of his soft jacket against my cheek, the sound of his voice, his smell. But I know I'll return to Birch Cove this summer, and maybe someday, forever.

Finally, I think about my mother, about how she's spent the last twenty-four hours since we returned from Teal Harbor

locked in her office, planning Hugh's memorial service, ham-
mering out the final details of the L.A. retrospective, obsessively
organizing and cataloging his work. She hasn't allowed herself
to cry, to mourn. I think she's afraid that once she starts, she'll
never be able to stop.

I want to reach out to her. I want to show her that she can
move on, that she can fashion a worthwhile life for herself with-
out Hugh Scully. But how? She still thinks of me as an outsider,
a child. And now, perhaps—because I helped Hugh escape to his
beloved island—as the enemy.

And then it occurs to me that if I can find a way to make
my own life worth living, to take the things that Hugh taught
me and put them into action, then perhaps my mother will see
that it's possible to carry on. Perhaps, in some small way, she
can learn from my example. At least it's a beginning.

I pause then, remembering the paints and brushes that Hugh
sent me to Sara's Studio to buy. They're still lying in my back-
pack, still wrapped in plastic, unopened. And suddenly I know
that my father didn't ask me to buy those paints simply because
he needed a way to get me off the island without a fight. That
was part of it, certainly. But there was more. He wanted me to
have them, to use them. They were meant for me.

I pick up my sketchbook and walk toward the barn doors. I
feel restless and excited, and it seems as if all those boxes inside
my head are flying open and the contents are blowing away. But
the peculiar thing is, I don't feel the need to stop them. I don't
even care. I've got other things on my mind now, other ideas.

I'm going to start painting.